The
Orser's
Promise

Megan Greenberg

Eloquent Books

Eloquent Books
An imprint of Strategic Book Group
P.O. Box 333
Durham CT 06422
www.StrategicBookGroup.com

ISBN 978-1-60860-857-7

Printed in the United States of America

Book Design/Layout by: Andrew Herzog

For Carley, Petra, Miranda Kestrel,
Seamus, Liam, Alayna, Bradley,
Mary, Wayne Jack Raven,
Lilith Rose, Rowan Moss
and all the kids inside

Author's Note
and Acknowledgements

Curious readers are invited to look up Alfred Noyes' *The Highwayman* or listen to the Loreena McKennitt or Phil Ochs versions.

My appreciation to Andrew Herzog and the team at Eloquent Books for all your help.

Many thanks to the many who fill my life with a love of words, and to the listeners and readers, without whom words are nothing.

Megan Greenberg
July 12th 2008 Vancouver, B.C.

Chapter 1

*S*creams of rage from the big house could be heard even in the stables, half a field away. Though more of an indistinct howl than a communication including words, the message was clear. Somebody was very, very angry. Somebody else had done something wrong, and Apt had a feeling it was her.

In the familiar stables, among the Orses nudging hay in sweet Spring sunlight, flies and beam faeries dancing lazily about the huge heads, Apt sat on a bale. Her awkward hands and forearms dangled longly between her skinny legs, one finger tufting a tear in the denim over her left knee where there was also a scab and a stain in the surrounding fabric.

Occasionally, the other workers of the big house would inquire after her clumsiness, wondering how she managed to injure and trouble herself as she did. The answer was that Apt managed nothing, like some extreme kind of non-interventionist monk meditating on non-involvement, her lack of action was so profound as to be sublime.

It's true that she was good with the Orses, however that was generally suspected to be because the Orses were good with her. Once, the chief Orser had witnessed two territorial males exchanging feed troughs the time Apt had put specially medicated feed for one into the trough of the other. They also seemed to make a point of not biting or kicking Apt. The Orses had looked after her for a dozen years and had few complaints, indeed seemed fond of the lass, favoring her with their low whickering and friendly behavior and obliging her with good health despite her well-meaning though inconstant care.

The keening rant flooding from the windows of the big house's second floor now grounded itself in three reverberant growls that seemed to rock Apt's bale with their basso profundo. The dancers quivered in the air.

"WHERE IS SHE?" The boss was mad this time, for sure. Was this really worse than the time Apt had hidden a favourite yearling in a secluded glade, telling the boss that it must've been stolen? Or when she had cleaned the stables adequately but not well, as was her wont, but then spent a day's work decorating the stables, including requesting (and getting, though the maid had since been fired) the parlor drapes, to create a romantic atmosphere for two Orses that were hoped to mate? In retrospect, it was easy to see that she'd gone just a little too far with these past enthusiasms, but they, like today's events, were all fuelled by good intentions. Apt wondered if she would someday view them with the same shamed eye.

It had just seemed so wrong, thought Apt, as she stood, arched and stretched in a crackle of multiphasic limbs. She yawned as she easily gathered her scant possessions. One hat, bundled around some sticks. One pair of socks that had been used as gloves so there were unraveling holes in them that were uncomfortable between the toes and were now awaiting use as gloves again in the colder season. Always worth taking along woolens, thought Apt, as she could always unpick and reknit them. Well, somebody could, anyway. That is, she could probably find a person who would do that if she tried, if she needed to.

It's already a warm Spring and I don't have to think about it, she thought as she unhitched her best Orse. He was still slightly winded from the hunt, but he was also her fastest. It was, in fact, he who had successfully sired on that night in the Sara Leo (as her boss had called it in disgust, surveying the elegant damask walls and flickering candlelight that really, the Orses had not minded). Her plan had worked, she thought, saddling and cinching under the muscular black belly, and after this Orse was done escaping her to the Antiquarian, he would return to his foal, to teach him more about running, carrots and other Orsey things.

It seemed that the clap of intent feet could be heard even above the Orse's initializing canter through the door, Apt astride.

*   *   *

It was a long ride to Pol's abode, providing ample time for Apt to review the troubling developments. The mighty beast rumbled over the land, a fast wind, happy with the earth under his hooves and Apt's knuckly, well-loved, often-apple-holding fingers stacked in his mane.

The boss was a hunter, a 'fine' hunter she had been called, and her especial field of expertise was in the elegant murder of small birds, especially birds that sang. One afternoon while selecting which Orse she would ride in the next day's hunt, the boss condescended to tell Apt,

"Once every four seasons, a certain species of twittering thrush migrates through these forests, drawn by the fruiting of the tingly berry bush. They are said to have the sweetest song because of their sweet diet.

I've heard them, and they're insufferable. Also, very tiny, and hard to hit. I haven't nabbed one yet, but this year I am certain of success. Apt!" she stopped the girl's hand as it was about to pour bony-growth-dissolver on the pommel of the boss' favourite white leather saddle. The boss sighed dramatically, avian animosity forgotten for the moment. "Apt. However did you get that name, girl?"

"You gave it me when I came."

"Did I?" Apt looked up to meet the boss' eyes, grey, flecked, looking not unkindly. It was the first time in many years Apt had seen them and the first time she'd seen them empty of anger. "Tell me."

"It seemed you were...in your cups. The villagers had brought me here when my family...went away. I was...tired."

"For goodness sake, girl, can you please be less elliptical?"

"Sorry..."

"Apt...oh Ferd, you've got me doing it. No more dots!"

"Yes, boss. When brought before you where you sat at the heart of some revel, I stumbled into a server, whose tray spilled into one of the visitors' laps! Who leapt up! Which caused the man at the other end of the bench to fall into the fire! He was unhurt but the pheasants fell among the ashes!"

"I think I recall. I was so angry but I couldn't stop laughing."

"Yes, and when you asked the villagers what they'd brought upon you—I remember you said it like that—"

"Yes, yes, go on."

"They said they'd brought me to be of service since my family was unable to care for me. You asked what they thought I was fit for. They responded that maybe I could have a place in the stable among the other dumb beasts and you said..."

"Oh. Aye, she'll be apt for that."

"And that's what they've called me ever since. You also mentioned that it was a fine name for rhyming, and your guests immediately contributed their witty suggestions."

"Rapt, Capped, Flapped, Mapped."

"Slapped, Lapped, Zapped, Trapped and..."

"Never mind," said the boss, "Whatever was said then, you've been here what, three, four years now?"

"Twelve, boss."

"I said never mind! Well, you're not inept, Apt, at least not with the Orses. I think I'll take this one on the hunt."

"This one" being the gorgeous dark animal that now bore her so effortlessly. The boss had good taste, anyway. Apt knew that she could have stayed, tried to explain why she'd done what she'd done, begged forgiveness and probably received it and been allowed to stay. It simply felt like far too much work to explain why she had packed the boss' equipment for the hunt with blinds, cushions, medical kit, wet-weather gear, a very nice lunch, nine styles of bows, fletching tools and a supply of five different kinds of feathers, three gauges of bowstring... and no arrows.

The boss was mad, and would likely stay mad for a long time. Apt thought it a suitable plan to shelter with her friend Pol who lived a comfortable distance away from the big house. The Antiquarian would be inclined to ask many questions about her change of circumstances, but could always be distracted by even the slightest interest in his researches. Apt knew she would be safe there from the boss' wrath only as long as she stayed hidden, for the trade between towns was

brisk and gossip-laden and a powerful woman would know Apt's whereabouts as quickly as the Antiquarian's neighbors did if she were to show herself.

They tended, Pol complained often and at length of his neighbors, to monitor his affairs, as though there was something untoward about the occasional small explosion, and his privacy was often imperiled by their curiosity about the shocking reek from the cellar or the fact that one day he had no livestock and the next there were to be seen several fluffy sheep on the

hillside and a cow in the barn, a barn that the villagers were sure had not been there before. Their interest was always less welcome than Apt's detached presence whose passive reception seemed to spur the Antiquarian to ever greater enthusiasm for his subject.

That at least had been Apt's experience on her last
visit with Pol, four years previous, when she had just
turned fourteen and Pol was recently returned from
the latest (the 11th) Ade. He had returned infested
with obscure wisdom from the latest victory over a
nomadic tribe of desert dwellers, who in their travels
had reached the Eem Ocean and themselves collected
lore from other nations who had traversed it. Pol was
replete with tales of invisible assassins, overflowing
with algorithms and impossible to shut up on the subject of the Undines of the Far Sea. Long into the night
had he tiraded, until finally, when Apt had refused to
keep awake a moment longer, no matter what fascinating things the desert people were doing with pre-
serving the dead, the Antiquarian had looked at her
kindly and said,

"You are tired, go to sleep, there are soft blankets
by the fire for you. You have become a wise woman."

"I haven't said a single thing since I got here."

"Hrm. I mean to say, we often learn more by listening than by speaking. I have always known you
would do well enough, since your parents honored me
with the request to conduct your naming ceremony
in the Green. When was that, again?" Pol settled into
his chair. "It would have been...let's see...seventeen
years ago, so just after I returned from the third Ade.
Oh, that was a journey for the telling! It was when the
Cold Prince had begun to ally himself with the Orangi
as well as the Ka'ri Tribes, despite their very complex

history, long-reaching really, and needing some pre-knowledge of the geographical terrain..."

Apt had gone to the soft blankets by the fire, though he had continued elucidating until the embers were banked low and she, half-sleeping, had wondered if he even knew she was here or if he was now pontificating for the sake of his new kitten's education. The Antiquarian had, in sudden silence, tucked the blankets closer around her chin and whispered,

"I will always be here for you and watch out for you. If you are ever in need, come to me."

And now she was, and had arrived. As she dismounted, it occurred to Apt that Pol was the only person in the world who knew her real name. She kept meaning to ask if he still remembered it, as she had forgotten it years ago.

The Orse, reluctant to stop running, needed much walking and brushing before he consented to be housed for the night next to the Antiquarian's three cows, one donkey and something like a bumpy Orse that spat at Apt as she closed the barn doors and took the path leading to where a window in the darkness glowed warm with light.

Chapter 2

At the round door of the Antiquarian's abode, Apt hesitated. While all appeared calm, she could sense a strange energy, and she kicked a few times at the base of the door rather than touch the ornate doorknocker. She kicked again and the Antiquarian appeared at the window.

"Try the knocker," he suggested.

"No," said Apt.

"It would be much nicer than kicking the door, do try."

"I'd prefer not, thank you." Apt replied evenly.

"The knocker is from Orangia, excellent crafting, a scene from the Spoodle wars, molded for extra resonance. I think you'll like it."

"I don't mean to be demanding, Pol, but could you open the door?" The head sighed and was withdrawn.

The figure that swung open the door with considerable effort a few moments later was a rounded, tweedy form with an abundance of whiskery. Apt noticed that his eyes, usually shining with the light of inspiration, only glinted dully as he peered at her.

"Well, it's you! You must come in. Would you like to try the doorknocker? No? Perhaps you would like to see my latest project?"

"Of course I would."

"It's just this, here, this doorknocker..." Stepping inside as though to put the matter to rest, Apt queried, "Any other projects? New discoveries?"

"Since I saw you last? A mere week? These things take time. I have had most remarkable success with this..."

"...Doorknocker, yes. Marvelous I'm sure." Actually, upon seeing the mammoth bundle of cables and cords that ran from the door to a generator on the kitchen table, it probably was marvelous, Apt thought. As was customary in the Antiquarian's abode, there was a lot to marvel at.

On her last visit, every surface had been buried in avalanches of books, flotillas of models and flocks of bell jars, leaving barely enough room to navigate the three-room cottage. In four years, the meager paths had built strata, and the journey from the door to the chairs by the hearth (at least, what she assumed to be the hearth as it was smoking, but so, she observed, were three other areas) was somewhat perilous. At one point Pol slipped beneath the surface and was gone for a few moments, then reappeared near a sturdy metal teapot which he lobbed gently in her direction. Apt being not quite herself, she caught it after the third bounce.

"Would you like to make some tea?" he asked. "A pinch from that basket and a bit of the powder from this one, but don't smell it until they're mixed or your nose'll fall off. I only ask because you're closest to the hot water," which, she noticed, was mysteriously boiling in a wicker basket hanging from the eaves near her head, "and it's such a long way back."

Apt followed his directions to a tea, and after a short excavation of the chairs, they were seated somewhat comfortably with their mugs.

"So tell me, what brings you here?" asked Pol.

"An Orse."

"And *why* did you get the Orse to bring you here?"

Apt recounted the story of her departure from the big house. When she told him of her incomplete provisioning for the boss' hunt he whooped with pleasure.

"Out for the twittering thrush with all her fancy friends and no arrows eh? Ha! She must have been livid. Well, I suppose you were right to come. You can stay here, a bit cozy but we'll get along I'm sure. Do you do laundry?"

"Everything I wash comes out smaller and pinker than it went in."

"Cleaning?" the Antiquarian looked hopeful. Apt looked around.

"I wouldn't want to disturb the processes of your experiments, Pol."

"Very sensitive of you, I'm sure. Hm, cooking is out."

"Why, what did you hear about my cooking?" Apt hadn't thought there'd been any survivors to speak of her last attempt at cuisine.

"No, no. My meals are all provided for me by the local Lattein monastery. A fellow comes by twice a day with something. I did them a favor and now they take care of me. I suppose I can share the food with you, though it'll be a stretch between you, me and the Chat."

"Pardon me?"

"French, a soft C, quiet T." The subject of discussion dropped onto the Antiquarian's questionable lap. Apt remembered the tiny kitten that bore no resemblance whatsoever to the fluffy, cushion-like being that was offering acupuncture treatment to Pol's bony knees. "We're working on languages. A limited attention span but good with vocabulary, this breed. We started with Cantonese but had a disagreement over the ninth tone and called each other various disagreeable things until we switched to French." The cat, purring, regarded Apt with sleepy, watchful eyes and a certain je ne sais quoi. "In the interests of immersion, while you're here, we'll need to speak only French."

"I don't speak French."

"That should cut down on the pesky arguments to which people sharing close quarters have such a pre-dilection. We'll start after this conversation. The Chat isn't really listening right now."

"How do you know?"

"I put cotton batting in his ears in case you were Mr. Angelford. He comes by to lecture me, never in French, on the merits of something called community involvement. I'm hoping he'll come by today, I've only just got the doorknocker working as I want it."

The sound of a bell put a topographically interest-ing smile on Pol's face. "That'll be our evening fare." Apt glanced out the almost-opaque window in time to catch a glimpse of a beige-cowled blur hurrying away while the Antiquarian placed a set of scales upon the table and began to measure portions of an unappetiz-ing pie. "Most pounds and most years gets the most mete." He scrutinized Apt's skinny frame. "How old are you now?"

"Eighteen." Apt replied. He adjusted the scales accordingly. Despite the specificity of his measure-ments, Apt noticed that her share was only marginally larger than that of the Chat, but said nothing.

The Antiquarian and Apt spoke as they ate the sim-ple and bland repast, during which it was made abun-dantly clear that Pol had become quite regimented in his lifestyle. There were rules for waking, sleeping, singing, walking, reading and most especially talk-ing. Between the stringent rules of his home and the knowledge that she could not leave it, Apt began to feel desperate.

"I don't want to intrude. Perhaps there is some-thing we can do to disguise me, so that I can leave you before I become a burden." Pol looked up, suspicious.

"What do you mean?"

"I remember after the 8th Ade you returned with some strange stories of face-changing..." Apt stopped, as the Antiquarian had risen and looked unusually upset.

"How dare you!"

"What did I say?"

"It wasn't the 8th, it was the 9th Ade! This kind of inaccuracy could throw everything out of balance!"

"My apologies, Pol. It was the 9th, then, when you returned with this information?"

"I never did! I don't know what you're talking about! C'est ca, assez, seulement francais." He pulled the cotton from the feline's ears (who made a sound quite a lot like "qwah?") and made his way laboriously from the room with the Chat in his arms.

Apt was puzzled. Where was her kindly Antiquar-ian, who had about twenty projects happening all the time and a tome's worth of information on any of them, who would discuss the most arcane, dangerous knowledge with virtually anyone? It was odd for him to be so guarded and intemperate. Much stranger that he would be speaking French.

In the morning the Antiquarian was much improved in spirit, and a spot of confusion about the douche notwithstanding, Apt's hopes for this arrangement were raised. They plummeted after a petit dejuner as his unpleasant and now strictly Gallic melancholy returned. At the end of a day spent trying to stay out of his way, made nervous and even clumsier by his impatience, Apt sat once more alone in a chair by the hearth.

The Chat, welcomed onto Apt's lap, allowed an absent-minded stroking of ears and forehead. They sat in silence for awhile, watching the flames burn purple and green in the grate. Apt sighed. A voice spoke. Apt realized the Chat was waiting for a response.

"I'm sorry, I don't speak French." The Chat stretched and yawned, saying,

"You might try the catacombs, if you'd like some space."

"O wise kitty, I'd quite forgotten!"

Apt had indeed forgotten the ancient burial grounds that stretched for acres below the Antiquarian's cottage, miles of quiet halls among the moldering bones, the reason Pol had made his home here. She knew there was an entrance to the catacombs from the cottage cellar, constructed in the days when they had been his greatest subject of study. Now, having exhausted their secrets, the Antiquarian seemed to remember them only in the records he'd kept.

Miles of corridors, crawlspaces and caves, a place to go to be alone and not have to hear the Antiquarian chastise her for a) dusting the chair before sitting or b) not dusting the chair before sitting, nor be called "great" only in the context of "cow of a girl", not to mention avoiding hearing the frequent phrase of "don't put your feet there!" She found herself quickly becoming fluent in Insult. He had also called her "Estupido" after the evening meal, which to Apt sounded not French at all, which perhaps made him a bit of an Estupido.

There had also been an argument about the cheval, whom Apt had freed after a gentle canter in the direction of the big house. Orses being famous for their orienteering skills, she knew he would return safely, but she missed his gentle strength the moment his flickering form vanished on the horizon.

The Antiquarian, refusing to relinquish his grumpy mood, had sequestered himself in his study all evening, so the idea of spending time among the very dead rather than the etiquette-dead was increasingly appealing. Apt wanted to thank the Chat for the suggestion, but it was gone.

*　　*　　*

The following day, a young eager sun rose and bright spirits reigned. Pol was pleased to hear of Apt's desire to see the catacombs, which she expressed by means of a few hand gestures and lack of facial expression. His moustaches twitched with visible relief.

It became Apt's practice to depart for the tunnels immediately after breakfast, which usually consisted of something called a pulse and the juice of an unrecognizable fruit that started sweet but ended bitter on the tongue, as, like the juice, the Antiquarian sat down sunny but became ever more vitriolic as the miserable meal was consumed, and there was nothing to be had from sticking around.

Pol was sometimes kind, and Apt thought she could see the curious, enthusiastic soul she'd known before. Weeks past there had been a day so hot she wished for a hat, and recalled her own, brought from the stables of the big house. As she retrieved it, she found the arrows, seven slender, red-tailed missiles that had not found the heart of a migrating songbird.

She had shown them to the Antiquarian in hopes of lifting his humor with thoughts of the unarmed hunter. He had laughed and was reminded of a bow he had, somewhere around. When, days later, he had found it (with help from the Chat) and given it her, Apt had felt touched. It was quite a beautiful thing, like ivory but living, tensile, and she was pleased to receive it of him who had been so ornery. Apt wondered if he was generally improved but he was back to bad humor over dinner, demanding that she go hunting her own self and improve the quality and quantity of their meals. She was through the door in the cellar before breakfast the next morning.

The catacombs were unsurprisingly quiet and, though the first few (most recently used) tunnels were a bit hard to take, the deeper reaches of the catacombs were more like an abandoned cathedral of the Very Small. After two moons of exploration and occasional rare surprises, she came to know well the peacefulness of the tombs. Surrounded by stillness Apt's mind allowed her the understanding that there would need to be a change, that something would have to happen. She could not hide forever.

*   *   *

What happened was this: Apt was returning through the catacombs by an unfamiliar route and became lost in narrower and narrower tunnels. When at last the hall began to slope up, she discovered that she was under the floor of the Antiquarian's study. She knew this from the sound of books being thrown around and landing just above her head, and Pol's grumbling. Though muffled, several phrases came through the boards clearly.

"She will not find it, she must not know." Slamming, creaking, a crash as though one of the overstuffed bookshelves had tipped, some cursing. "It must be secret, I will lock it away." There was a groan, as of a sticky drawer, another slam, and a click. Whatever Pol was protecting, Apt's curiosity was now inflamed.

That evening, as she sat with the Gato (the household was apparently done with French and had moved on), she began to grit her teeth with frustration. Earlier in the day, Apt had offered to tidy the study in hopes of finding the key to the locked drawer of Pol's desk, but despite many hours of hazardous labor, she had found nothing. It was over dinner that a clink on the rim of Pol's soup bowl had alerted her to the presence of a key, strung around his neck on a silver thread, chiming the chipped bowl as he hunched protectively over his much larger portion. Apt was certain that this was the key she sought, but how was she ever to retrieve it? As she wondered by the fireside, the Gato gazed at her with something like compassion and enquired after her trouble.

"He's so different!" Apt cried. "He was never this cantankerous before, never so untrusting. The Antiquarian I knew would have jumped at the chance to experiment with odd spells, especially if he knew it would help, or potentially explode. But now, he is so..."

"Grumpy?" suggested the Gato. "Ill-mannered? Intolerant, bad-natured, petulant, querulous?"

"You've a good grasp of synonyms."

"I'm just happy to have someone to speak English to. Really, he thinks I need language skills. I think he should try one of the more obscure dialects of Tabby, or Felino-Siamese. Then he'd know what language study was all about. And he thought the ninth tone of

Cantonese was a challenge! There are fifty-seven tones in Siamese." The Gato demonstrated a few variations. "Now that's a language!"

"Perhaps I'll make a study of it someday." Apt mused, uncovering her ears. "If I have to stay here, I'll probably learn everything in the whole world." The Gato rolled onto its back, inviting tummy-rubs, and said,

"There's far more in the world than what he has collected of it." The Gato's eyes closed as Apt massaged its belly.

"I wouldn't know, I've never been anywhere, know nothing of anything save what he's taught me of his travels...and Orses, I do know Orses. But that's not enough, it won't help me."

The Gato suddenly and perversely attacked and attempted to disembowel the hand it had been appreciating but a moment ago. Apt could have told it that the hand has no bowels, but the Gato was enjoying itself. It stopped and was instantly in a prim, seated pose, washing its paws. After a thorough investigation of the spaces between its extremely pink toes, it whispered,

"I can get the key for you." Apt felt a rush of catitude (being grateful to a cat) but also doubtful.

"But you're his pet." Ears back on the belligerent, triangular head, it regarded Apt greenly.

"I'm whose, now?"

"I mean, um, why would you help me?" The Gato relaxed.

"I would do it out of the goodness of my heart, and because I hate to see a maiden so upset."

"Really?"

"No. I'd do it so that there's more food to go around."

"Oh. Well, thank you, I'd be most grateful." They were quiet, and then the Gato, looking worried, said,

"He is different. He has changed much, and is much changeable."

"Maybe he's just getting older."

"No. This angry confusion seems to have another source. His natural capacity for being cantankerous could not equal his current tetchiness. It's worse after he eats. I don't know if I'll be able to live with him."

"Because he's so irritable?"

"And because he does not share the food fairly. That's a bad symptom." Apt looked the Gato in the eyes, brown meeting green, the weight of a promise between them.

"If you help me, I will try to find a way to bring the Antiquarian back to his normal state of being."

"A bit further past normal with a noted generosity towards animal companions and I'll be most pleased to accept your offer. You've got what humans call a good heart."

"Would an animal not speak of a good heart?"

"Oh, yes, but it's usually more of a taste-and-texture thing. The closest animal equivalent would be to say you smell good."

"Do I smell good, little cat?"

"No, of course not, humans smell worse than anything."

"Worse than garbage?"

"Garbage is perfume compared to the way humans smell."

"That's awful!

"You have no idea," the Gato seemed to smile, "but it's not your fault. Something to do with the frontal lobe, I think. All those morals and nonsensical rules, they stink. A bit over-evolved if you ask me." Just then, the Antiquarian emerged from his room.

"Where have my glasses gone, did you take them? I bet you misplaced them again, I told you..." Before rising from the chair, Apt whispered,

"Gracias, amigo." and heard the Gato's purring reply.

"De nada..."

The Antiquarian was napping before the hearth when the Gato appeared at Apt's side. It began to retch and gagged up the key on its long filament.

"You didn't have to eat it." Apt remarked, surveying the pool of disgusting mess.

"Mrph...hard not to. Thought it might be a mouse."

"A metal mouse?"

"It had a tail. Just take it, use it, get what you need and go before dinner."

She did. At the bottom of the bottom drawer, beneath an envelope marked with a date two years past and the words 'URGENT, Kingdom Taxes, File Immediately', she found what she was looking for, a folio of papers bearing the heading "Trancemogrification Among the Alpen Easterns." She replaced the folio with a note that said she'd return it and the key when she could. Then Apt gathered her hat, arrows, bow and spare pair of socks, decided to leave the gloves behind, and disappeared for the last time into the catacombs.

*   *   *

In the next two days, Apt ate only the dried fruit offerings left with more recent burials of followers of the Temple of the Sugar Glider, licked damp lichen for water, and experimented with the simple instructions found in the folio.

There was more to read than she had time for. The changes required massive effort and concentration, both of which were not in Apt's usual fields of expertise. They were also fairly painful, and she hoped that if Pol could hear her yells, he would think them merely restless ghosts. She could hear his own howls upon discovering the missing folio, and floods of angry Greek, French, Latin and English flooded the catacombs and echoed through the tunnels. From what she understood of his ranting, he had now completely forgotten that she'd ever been there, and the theft was being attributed to alien visitors.

Thus reassured of her successful escape, Apt spent many hours in sheer wrong-headedness (a pink eraser, the grille from an unfamiliar type of carriage which had the advantage of two bright lamps for eyes, a red carnation, a too-beautiful and, though Apt knew it not, instantly recognizable copy of a famous painting) before she finally, with the help of a mirror in someone's burial goods, saw a face that she could work with. Her own red hair was now a medium brown, curls had straightened, pale skin had darkened, brown eyes were now a pale green much like the Cat's. These changes pleased her and she knew they'd protect her.

Apt was certain now that she could go into the world without fear, and a burning desire seized her. Her quest calling with urgency undeniable, Apt struck off in the direction of the nearest public house.

Chapter 3

Bitter enemies will still meet and drink together with careful civility at the pub. Apt wondered as she entered the Terrible Boar if she would ever again find herself and the Antiquarian deep in laughter-filled conversation over a couple of ales.

Tribal warriors, landsknights, entertainers and... er...ladies filled the smoky room. Clamor, clangor and clash, of glasses, horns and steins, good-natured arguments and coldly polite conversation rose about Apt dizzyingly. Angry voices began to lift above the din, and tension suffused the air as two barbarians rose from their benches to glower at their companions, a pair of cloaked and hooded rangers.

Apt approached the bar, where a rotund, dark-haired beauty meditatively polished an immense, mangled silver mug.

"Help you?" the woman asked. Apt gestured at the fearsome foursome that seemed to be positioning themselves for a dance.

"Will there be a fight?" she asked. The woman coolly reviewed the scene.

"Aye, no doubt. Are you afeared, lass?"

"No worse than spooked Orses. I was wondering if I might help you clean up after? For a beer now?" The woman smiled and drew two small tankards of ale and poured a glass of something murky and caustic-smelling.

"Two beer, and a bit of the house spirits, I think this'll be a messy one." Apt drank one beer to brace herself for the spirits, which she tossed back praying for mercy and quickly followed with the remaining ale. Stars spun. If these were spirits, they were low, and could probably double as bony-growth-dissolver. They might even be useful cleaning up after the fight. She staggered against the bar as the woman caught her at the elbow.

"There now, lass. They've got a bit of a kick."

"No...worse than spooked Orses." Apt groaned. The woman settled her on a stool that tipped alarmingly. Seated, things settled, though her stomach after weeks of simple food, and little enough of that, demanded to know what outrage she'd perpetrated on it.

The barkeep extended a calloused, meaty hand.

"Bess." she said. Apt took it, clasped.

"Bess the landlord's daughter?"

"Now just Bess the landlord."

"But that is a..." Apt began, gesturing to a deep red, ribbon-bedecked braid in the publican's silver star-light-streaked midnight hair.

"...a love knot. Yes, old habits die hard, as they say. Especially on a night like this, when the moon is a ghostly galleon and the road..."

"Is a ribbon of moonlight over the purple moor?"

"...aye." sighed Bess.

"Did he ever come back? Riding, riding, riding?"

"Nay, haven't seen him, though he did say he'd come to me."

"By moonlight?"

"Yea, though Hell should bar the way. But you know men, dearie. All sweet talk and promises, but when it comes down to it...you might want to duck." Apt bent as a flagon whirled past her head and dented itself on the wall. She accepted Bess' invitation to join her behind the bar where they crouched, occasionally peeking out at the melee.

One enormous warrior, all lime-hardened hair, maddened eyes and greasy leather armor, was attempting to use a rather skinny knight as a bow staff. The knight's elbows and feet made him an excellent weapon as he was spun. Every bench had been over-turned and some had been enlisted as large cudgels. The thwack and smack of drunken fists resounded.

A diminutive man wearing only a pair of dark paja-mas was with bare hands and feet disarming and ren-dering unconscious any fighter unwise enough to place himself within reach of the small man's limbs, which seemed to move faster than the eye could fol-low. A smelly stack of would-be assailants piled up around him.

After what seemed like hours, the noise faded, and only groans could be heard. The pub looked like an angry child's toybox and the small, quick man carefully picked his way across the littered floor to the bar. Bess poured him a glass of something and commended him as the fighter drank it with small, elegant sips.

"Any fatalities tonight?" Bess asked. The man smiled, eyes creasing.

"Not from me. The clumsy ones, they may have assisted some souls into the next life, but I remember what you said."

"The dead drink not, neither do they pay."

"Yes, and when this lot," he indicated with a bladed hand the heap of ten or so warriors he had felled, "awaken, they'll be both hungry and thirsty. For to come so close to the next world and not touch it makes the soul hunger more for all the pleasures of this one. Your taps will flow, your larders will empty...and the ladies will be busy tonight." He eyed Apt with a grin.

"She's no lady, Chen." Bess warned. As the publican settled accounts, Apt began to clean up.

First the bodies needed to be taken out; for this she requested the help of the giant warrior and his human bowstaff, both of whom were remarkably unscathed. Next the unconscious but living needed to be put to one side, then the rushes needed to be refreshed. Here, that meant simply scattering another layer of sweet broom over the gore-encrusted ones below. It was a harder task getting the blood off the walls, especially as she kept getting interrupted to bring trays of drinks and food to awakening patrons. Chen's predictions came to pass and Bess and Apt had their hands full.

"Is it always this busy after a fight?" Apt asked breathlessly, arms aching under the weight of laden trays.

"Aye," replied Bess, moving at a quick pace between the ale taps and the kitchen. "Nothing like it to remind men they're mortal with mortal men's needs. Others will come, be drawn to it as if by smell, and they will later claim to have fought bravely and will take other men's tales as their own. By tomorrow, several of these men will be giant warriors, and at least three will have become Chen. Happens every time. Every night. At least once."

"D'you ever miss peacefulness?" asked Apt.

"Violence everywhere, miss, angry people everywhere too. Too many fellows spoiling for a bust-up. Best to be in the midst of it and have it between four walls with Chen on payroll than be out in the world expecting peacefulness." Bess laughed.

As the evening progressed, the mood lightened. Laughter was heard from every table save one; several monks, huddled around a lone candle and nursing the same beers they'd started the night with, spoke in gloomy whispers. Apt paused to enquire after their trouble.

One monk intoned with the age-old honesty a bartender's question may evoke,

"Our King's favourite wife is ill, too ill. We fear for her, and for the kingdom, for if Lentdemain should pass away from us, the King will surely follow for love of her. The factions in our land are eager for this to occur, for one of them would then seize the throne and it is only the King who truly understands the worth of our work on his behalf. The warlords are faithless heathen, and would pillage our abbeys and disband our brotherhood. We would be exiled." Apt agreed that this was most distressing.

"If I come across anything that will help you, I will send word." Apt declared. Most of the monks laughed dourly, one said "Oh, a bargirl, yes, our savior, some help." but one, smiling, gave her the name of the brotherhood and told her of the symbol by which she would recognize its members, a red rose and white lily entwined with each other.

"Your efforts are worth as much as our own in this matter and the kindness of your offer lends strength to our struggle. D'you hear of anything that could save our mistress, I pray you, remember us." Apt promised she would.

It was then that the publican clapped her hands, announcing that the evening's arts would soon commence. Amid the bellicose cheers, she grabbed Apt in passing.

"You can stay, if you've nothing pressing. The tumblers are amusing and the dancers are worth watching, if only for the lightness their step brings to a heavy heart. Most special of all, my own son, who is recently returned and a great poet, will perform for us. You've been a fine help, and have more than earned an evening's revel and a night's sleep. In the morning, you can tell me of your plans, and I will assist you if I can."

Apt felt a painful flash in the corners of her eyes and wondered if it was the after-effects of the turbid liquor she'd drunk. She accepted gratefully, eyes down at the already-dirty fresh rushes below her feet, feeling the soft caress of the barkeep's warm smile upon her.

*   *   *

Bess was right, Apt thought, she had earned a night of relaxation. She'd seen tumblers and dancers at the big house, having been pressed into kitchen service, but freed to observe the entertainment after the feast was demolished by the boss' guests. The boss had commended the acrobats and dancers whose steps and tricks demanded massive, graceful strength, but the poets and musicians, except as they supported the dancers, were viewed with a dismissive eye, and all singers were banned. If the art wasn't physically dangerous, the boss found it not amusing in the slightest, so Apt had been left with the impression that poetry and storytelling were wastes of voices that could otherwise have been employed for hymn-chanting or perhaps announcing honoured guests at a soiree.

Apt enjoyed the performances, especially the audience participation. The giant had been invited to balance one of the acrobats on his hand, though it was really the acrobat who did the balancing, her tiny foot almost engulfed in the scarred paw, and she served as the fulcrum for her partners, swinging them through the air. The crowd was rapt, holding its breath as the tumblers pirouetted on nothing at all, cheering when small, slippered feet lit again on the open space before the bar.

The audience was also most pleased with the animal acts, among them costumed dogs that climbed ladders, leapt though hoops and marched with regimental precision, as well as the mimes, who appeared to be surrounded by scenes, props and dramas that they alone could see, impeccable gestures illuminating the invisible until those in the audience themselves began to smell the roses, jumped to catch the hat a wind had whisked away, saw the beautiful woman that made the mimes' jaws drop and hearts beat like trapped birds against their black-striped shirts.

The crowd, considering its constituents, was unquestionably well behaved, until the poets began their segment.

The first poet, an odd, pale sort with a grinding note to his voice, declaimed the likeness of his love to the Autumn, how the beloved, like the year, was growing old and dying. Apt was certain this was not the son Bess had spoken of, as she would have no doubt advised him in plain terms of the dubious quality of his work. His phrasing was unfortunately, accidentally humorous and the crowd began to chuckle about fallen women, quickly losing patience with the delicacy of verse presented. Frustrated, the performer sped through his inane couplets and, noting the presence of some aerodynamic-looking fruit in the hands of a couple of vocal critics in the front row, departed.

A Lady Poet, reviewing the assemblage with disdain, began the first of several French poems. She was tolerated for longer than the first had been on the grounds that she might be saying something naughty, it sounded well and she was pleasant-looking, but impatience again rose in the pack. They demanded English, to which the Lady Poet replied that she should have expected no better of such a rabble. As the audience did not take kindly to being spoken to thusly, the Lady Poet's own underdeveloped tumbling skills were tested as she somersaulted below the arcing tomatoes.

Apt was yawning and the crowd was restive when the last performer stepped into the pool of light furnished by bright lanterns near the bar. The giant called out,

"Being the whelp of the barkeep will help ye none, do your rhymes not improve the quality of fare, we've tomatoes with your name on them."

"And a potato." added a rodent-faced fellow at the giant's side. Apt recognized one of the former victims of the human bowstaff, now seemingly recovered enough to wish to redeem his pride by assailing another's, especially another who appeared unarmed.

The poet turned to face the hecklers, a steady, comfortable grin on his face.

"Tough crowd." he observed, to which the audience responded with raucous cheers. He waited until the din quieted. Then he waited until the pub was silent. Then he waited until a fist was raised, cradling a leaky tomato, when at last he spoke, in a voice that seemed larger than his body could carry,

"The Winning of Lentdemain." The name of the realm's most famous courtesan, the implication that there might be some ribaldry to it, as well as the combined glower of the table of monks, caused a hush to settle.

This true, receptive quiet, different than the ominous silence that had met the previous poets' attempts, called Apt's attention away from the friendly circus dogs with whom she'd been amusing herself, and she looked upon the poet for the first time.

If anyone had cared to ask Apt what she thought of poetry, she would have allied her opinion with her previous boss' take on the merits of this art, that people should not be paid simply to talk, and that memory-work deserved even less compensation, but as the poet delivered, with flawless rhythm and intonation a tale of tragic love, Apt felt she would give the riches of a kingdom to have this wordsmith continue.

And he was very pretty, which went a long way in Apt's estimation. The only men she'd been around were the unavoidable ones, beery, flatulent banquet guests, other Orsers as malnourished and smelly as she, and the old master craftsmen in charge of the shoeing and outfitting of Orses, who saw her not at all, as she was A) not rich and B) two-legged. A beautiful man was a thing unknown to her, she knew only enough to say that he was indeed beautiful, building this judgment from what she'd seen in the portraits and tapestries of the big house. The princes and lords of those depictions also had the poet's dark hair, curling loose to broad shoulders, the same lambent skin, the same commanding stance informed by muscular, breech-clad legs. A power shone from him as from them, but in those men it spoke of high birth and a benevolent artist who conveniently forgot about the more, say, unpleasantly emphatic of characteristic features. The poet owed his radiance only to the strength in his spine, the depth of his gaze and his words, which, as Apt listened, shivered her flesh like winter and summer fighting.

She could see Bess in him, in his hair, health and confident voice that spun itself out into the room as a web, trapping his listeners among sticky cross-strands of clever rhymes and a somehow-original way of speaking what was already deeply familiar. Apt wondered if his father had been the one Bess spoke of, if the unknowable man had bequeathed to his unknown son his rakish smile, irresistible charm and silver tongue as legacy in place of the yellow gold he had promised Bess but proved unable to deliver.

Whatever his composition, the poet's audience sat spellbound, forgetting even to drink. Circus dogs stealthily slipped meat from ignored plates without reprisal, the mottled (but clean) walls seeming to be magicked away and replaced with the sights and sounds, even the perfumes of a romantic kingdom far away. Apt fell deeper into the oaken heart of the poet's voice.

He held the crowd in one gloved hand and stroked it gently with the other for the course of two more pieces that despite their length, sped by as though he had uttered them in one long, full breath. When complete, he declined the appeal for more from the clamoring throng, smoothly making his way among the well-wishers to a table where several beers (the crowd had liked him too much to stand him any of the house spirits) awaited him.

Apt felt a discomfort in her abdomen that was relieved by her resolve to approach his table, which she did, more awkward than ever. As she was about to ask his name and tell him of her admiration, she noticed that he was already surrounded by admirers of the female variety, women who had come for the evening's entertainment and were now planted around him like a garden of silken flowers, pearls among their coiffures glimmering like dew on unfurling petals, delicate faces turning as though towards the sun. Close enough to overhear these women saying to him the same words that rested on the tip of her own tongue in a face that was more like a weed than a rose, Apt knew there was nothing she could offer him, nor of him ask. One woman, festooned with swathes of light pink silk, jewels dripping from her dainty hand as she cupped the poet's velvet-sleeved arm, promised to be at the poet's next performance the following night at a pub called the Open Hart. Silently, Apt swore the same.

Chapter 4

"*L*ast call!" shouted Bess. There were only a dozen or so patrons left in the Terrible Boar, most having adjourned upstairs with the ladies or returned to their wives with exaggerated tales of prowess, but the few remaining made up for in volume what they lacked in numbers, and Apt and Bess dealt with the many large drink orders, that is, most of the patrons were ordering many large drinks. Bess was explaining to one sullen villager why she was prevented by provincial health laws from serving the house spirits in the amount he'd requested.

"Blind drunk is blind drunk! I don't need to be able to see!" he protested. "In fact," he said blearily, "I don't think I'll want to see myself on the morrow, nor my wife's face when I stumble home. If the drink should kill me so much the better, it'd save her the trouble." Apt gathered empty plates and mugs as Bess remonstrated with him, and by the time he'd finally been convinced, perhaps more by the brawny arms crossed sternly over Bess' bosom than by her sound arguments, the place was deserted, and sufficiently tidy. Bess looked around approvingly.

"You've done a fine job." she said, patting Apt's stiff shoulder. "Have you ever thought of going into this line of work?" Apt stared at the publican, amazed.

"I'd not thought of it, this being my first time in a public house."

"Well, you carried yourself fair enough. D'you have a trade, or are you meant to marry?" Apt had never considered this question, so hedged on the answer.

"Does one stand in the way of the other?"

"There's some'd say Aye, some'd say Nay, but the first tends to be men and the second is women. Then there's the women who say it's trade enough to wife a man, and the men who say there is no suitable trade for women but the work of a wife."

"What do you think, Bess?" The landlord smiled at Apt, and elected to answer her own question rather than Apt's.

"I think you've a trade, that you fell into and never climbed out of, and if you're ever to marry I think you'd do it the same. What is it you do, when you're not playing angel of mercy for a busy barkeep?"

"I'm an Orser."

"A what, now?"

"An Orser, I care for the Orses."

"...You mean an Ostler."

"They're not called Ostles. I'm an Orser."

"They're not much called Orses either, except for those who drop their Aitches. Say it, 'Horses'."

"Orses."

"Huh...orses."

"Yes, Orses."

"Let it be. Are you all in?" Bess inquired.

Apt looked down at her stained tunic and up again, quizzically.

"I think so."

"Tired, I mean. You must be ready for bed." Apt yawned in agreement.

"I could sleep for a whole night. Where are your stables?"

"Stables? Nonsense. I said bed and bed you shall have. Tonight at least you'll have some cotton between you and the straw. And a bath. But you'll have to draw the water."

"I've seen beds, they look very comfortable, and I'd like to try one. But as for the bath...I have two questions."

"Never been in a bed! That's much worse than never having been in a pub! What are your questions?"

"Will it make me sick?"

"A bath? It'll make you sick of bathing in icy streams and dirty troughs, no more. Your other question?"

"I'm not a very good artist, maybe you could draw it?"

Bess hid her laugh behind a handkerchief and led Apt upstairs to the best room in the house.

"It's not much, but it's more than the other rooms... see, you can stand up in it and everything!" Apt looked around at the neat, soft bed, the bathtub, the carpets on the floor as though in disbelief that this could be for her. She was permitted to pour pot after pot of steaming, clean water into the tub and offered soap and a handful of lavender blossoms whose scent rose like Apt's incredulity until both evaporated in the heaven of her first bath.

Apt woke in water the temperature of the glacial stream that was her usual fare. The soak had eased her sore muscles and put her to sleep; only Bess' knock roused Apt enough to lift herself from the tub and drop, dripping, upon the cushy mattress. She'd meant to enjoy the sensation of her first bed, but she was just too tired for anything but the thought that when we work very hard to earn something, we are often unable to immediately appreciate it because of the effort it took to get there, before she fell asleep.

And woke, startled, to an absence of familiar fug and clouding Orse-breath. The bed, fluffy and smothering, confused her body and she struggled with it restlessly until finally she rose, opened her door a bit and clicked her tongue twice. Circus dogs slipped from the room where their human lay in a stupor and came to join her. In the morning, Bess found Apt curled peacefully on the floor in a pile of snoring dogs.

*   *   *

Breakfast in the pub was a mellow affair. The doors to the garden were open, admitting sunlight and the occasional chicken. A gentle breeze with rosemary on its breath swept around the room, which was now a very different place from the public house of the night before.

Apt joined Bess at a table whose scars shone in the daylight. Bess offered a cup of the same hot burnt bean juice she was drinking and they sat companiably as Apt studied the words roughly carved in the blond wood, asking Bess what they meant when she could not understand. This was often, and the proprietress was becoming increasingly flustered.

"No, you see, in this context it's an adjective. Over here it's a noun, and this one...er...this would be a verb."

"That's a good word!"

"Yes, it's very multi-purpose, but don't go spreading this good word around."

"Why? Is it not suitable for girls to use?"

"As suitable as any other, and more than some. But if you say it too much, it loses its power."

"So it's magic?"

"It can be, in the right circumstances. It's wiser to use it advisedly, so that others don't judge you wrongly."

"How could they judge me wrongly?"

"You see, you're a bright person, learned, you read and speak well. This word can bring your language low, and they might think you base-born"

"But I am base-born. That would not be a wrong judgment."

"Or impolite."

"The boss always said I was."

"Why would she say that of such a helpful lass?"

"She said I asked too many questions, and did not know my place."

"Hah!" Bess exclaimed. "As if she'd know what your place should be. This boss sounds like a woman I know, a hunter, with as little regard for those around her as the birds she shoots. Less, perhaps." Apt thought it was time to change the subject.

"Your son is a very talented poemer...not that I know anything about poeming."

"Poet, and poetry, dearie. Where did you learn your English?"

"From the...just picked it up, I suppose."

"Must've picked it up from someone who didn't have a lot of love for the belles-lettres."

"I don't know if he loves the bellytree or not, but he sure knew a lot of words."

After a moment, Bess looked inquiringly at Apt.

"What's your favorite?" Apt looked blank for a moment, then said with excitement,

"UNDINE! I used to think it meant to throw up one's food after eating, like undo or unravel are opposites of do and ravel. But now I know it means a sea faery."

"And why does that please you so?" asked Bess. Apt ticked the reasons off on her fingertips.

"One, because there are sea faeries and they have a name, and that name is Undine. Two, because it sounds like them, undulate, underwater, undecided..."

"Undecided?"

"...yes, 'cause they spend so much time in the water they're wishy-washy. "

"Ah, it's onomatopoeic." Apt looked nonplussed. "It means a word that sounds like a sound. Like 'tlot-tlot' sounds like a horse's galloping hooves."

"It does not. But Lmnopayick is a good word too. Three, it makes me happy to know the sea has faeries too. Some people say they are imaginary, but P...I know someone who's seen them. Maybe I'll see them too, with all the adventures I'm having now."

"Mayhap you will. What is your next adventure, lass?" Apt became quiet. Her eyes, when they met Bess', were wide.

"My next adventure will be going to the Open Hart." she smiled secretly. The quality of Apt's smile twitched the edges of Bess' lips as she replied,

"That's a long journey, half a day at least, through some of the most briganded territory in the county. Travelling alone, unguarded..."

"I have a bow and arrows." Apt defended sharply.

"O, well, then I'm sure nothing bad will happen to you." Apt heard Bess' sarcasm, and her eyes narrowed.

"I can take care of myself. I'm very grateful for your hospitality, but I think I should be on my way." She rose, and Bess followed.

"You're tough stuff, aye, but the journey will go easier with Anthem. She's a good old donkey who knows the way and will find her way back to me when you've safely arrived. Please take her with my thanks." Apt softened, and hugged Bess, who, after a pause, asked, "How do you feel about unsolicited advice?"

"Unsolicited advice is immoral," Apt declared. "but if you wish to give me some I'll receive it."

"All right. Three things," She ticked them off on her own fingers. "one, that I must needs remember myself (which is why most advice is given), no one's judgment of you should ever matter more than your own."

"Got it."

"Two: My beloved son, who truly is a great poet, is not yet a great person. Do not confuse the two."

"And the third?"

"Un-deen. To rhyme with between."

Apt again thanked the landlord, received her thanks in return, and was poised to go when she heard,

"Wait, girl!" Apt paused.

"After all this, I still don't know your name!" Bess said. Apt shook her head.

"That's all right. Neither do I." Declining to explain, she went to meet Anthem and begin her journey to the Open Hart.

*   *   *

The journey was easier with Anthem, as Bess had promised. The road was level, the weather clement, and whatever brigands or roustabouts might have been interested in her as a target were put off by the donkey's incessant, obnoxious and very loud braying, which commenced when Apt mounted and did not end until she got off the old swayback at the sign of the Open Hart. Anthem (and now Apt knew whence had come the name, she could have also been named

Fanfare, or even Blat) turned back the way she'd come, without so much as a nuzzle, leaving Apt alone at the door.

She'd beat the poet and his entourage by hours, as she'd been up since dawn and they, according to Bess, would sleep past noon. Apt went off to explore the countryside, being now further afield than she could have ever dreamed, and full of curiosity.

She returned as the last of the sun's rays were falling over the gabled roof of the inn, its outbuildings and stables. The Open Hart being much larger than the Terrible Boar, Apt reasoned there'd be even more of a mess to clean up, so she bravely entered, sought out the innkeeper and offered her services which he accepted eagerly. Then Apt clarified what her services would entail and he, less enthusiastically but still warmly, agreed that she could have a meal, the night's entertainment and a place in the stables for sleeping in return for the same work she'd done for Bess.

Even though the inn was packed with people and she was kept flying with food and drink for the guests, every minute of waiting for the poet's performance seemed to drag on and on. The time-candle burned away the hours with excruciating slowness, and every act and turn in the show, even the most appealing, held no interest for her.

Apt wondered why time had become so slow, why everything was happening as though through taffy, stretching long and longer. She had not experienced this, she realized, because she had not in her memory ever looked forward to anything, that usually the next thing that would happen was going to be a bad, or at least an unpleasant thing.

As a consequence she'd become much better at learning to enjoy what was happening now rather than put any confidence in the thought that the future could be worth being hopeful of. As the hours broke down into eternal minutes, it became clear to Apt that she was doing something she was very new to, and that thing was wanting.

> *I want it to be now. I want to run my fingers*
> *through that voice again and hear it really*
> *hear it really want it*
> *be*
> *now,*
> *want to be told*
> *now recited tickled, stymied and crazed like a*
> *vase is crazed when I bump into it with my*
> *sharp left elbow*
> *sty-me'd, to be*
> *down in the dumps*
> *find me there want*
> *to be found be*
> *now*

But it wasn't. It was still later.

A trio of clowns, mad, sad and glad revealed themselves under the tawdry velveteen wireframe of the Orse they had made of themselves, now! Not now, now the now of a sylph who sang, magnificently and so, so sorrowingly in an unidentified tongue, concluding with a note that held in the air the breath of the dozens of people and others in the room, releasing to inhale now! Not now. Now table 17 needs an Egg-over, 2 clams on salt, a Jooliebaby and 3 banana martinis, the soldiers in the corner need 24 pints, 12 ale, 12 stout because they want to play drafts, and check

the outhouse, patrons are refusing to go in there now
the masks spin, voices hoarse from laughing, shouting,
drinking, fried potatoes pelting the magician whose
doves join forces, seize with their claws the hat con-
taining the hidden bunny and fly up and out through
the hole in the thatch, like large stars getting smaller
amid true stars that are only pinholes in the smoke

now rising, the magician plumes his way out in a burst of purple fog and clean up the fried potatoes

now,

not now, it will never be now, it's only been ten minutes, thought Apt, as she dumped table 12's Flaming Chili casually upon a hand that had just reached for her backside. It still not being now, Apt considered this occurrence. Men, she noticed, and some women, were looking at her a little like she'd been looking at the time-candle, as though it would exist best if devoured utterly. Did the face she'd finally selected attract too much attention? Could it have something to do with being clean? She sniffed herself. It was gone, a smell so much her she hadn't even known it was there. Apt was consummately devoid of Orse scents.

Many sequins later, still not now, now an impressionist who impersonated people with whom the crowd was unfamiliar to a disastrous but ironically humorous end giving way to the candle burning at eleven and, now?

To whistles and cheers stepped the poet into stage light.

Now.

Apt, who had worked harder than any of the regular staff, now took a beer from her tray, passed the tray itself to a random table, and sat herself comfortably on the floor under table 3, avoiding feet.

Tonight he had a black harp, dully reflective and bending illumination, that vibrated with his voice almost but not perfectly, which was perfect, and the songs were very gay. He barded to a sea of smiling faces.

Apt was not smiling.

Blinked and done, that now was almost a nothing it had become then so fast.

She employed her newly acquired public-house maintenance skills for the remainder of the evening, for the poet's performance was the last of the night (the innkeeper knew how to stack the deck) and in all the celebration and high spirits some feelings got hurt, and then some noses and other parts. Luckily, the lime-haired warrior and his ratly accompanist were there to hear the poet again, and they once more lent Apt a hand with the best of Bonhomie (that being the town they were in, and the best of the locals were mostly among the rushes, and they did need a hand, some of them needed a whole arm, but there are limits to cooperative endeavors). The cleanup was extensive, and by the time Apt was dismissed for the night her only want, though she was still having one, was for a bed of hay and a blanket made from the sleepbreath of Orses.

From which she awoke, in terror. Furious shouts meant to raise the inn's inhabitants had raised Apt as well as every hair on her. The Orses were upset, and this made her madder than the rude awakening.

"Bring out the girl!" the voices demanded.

There were a lot of them, Apt saw through the boards, and they had fire. Not unwarranted, as the roads were dark and the moon was obscured, but the quality of the fire was unpleasant. It was big, and on long sticks, so as to reach things. Flammable things. Apt regarded the hayloft and thatch roof appraisingly.

The mob (definition: more than one human with big fire on long sticks) repeated their demand. The inn's guests and staff peered out. The innkeeper himself, turtle-like, daringly extended his face beyond the window frame to say,

"Yes? Which sort would you like?"

"The girl with the bow!" roared the mob's leader.

"No girls with beaux around here, sir. Nope. Don't hold with those kinds of things myself."

"A stranger."

"Ah." breathed the innkeeper.

"WHERE IS SHE?" Déjà vu, thought Apt. The innkeeper has no reason to give me away, they wouldn't expect that I'd be in the stables and he doesn't know I have a bow, I'm probably-

"Oh, right, her! She's in the stables, feel free. Back to bed everyone, our apologies for the temporary inconvenience."

-safe.

Oh, advisedly, thought Apt.

Before when she had run, she had done it to avoid punishment for having tried to save some lives. Now, she did the exact opposite for the same reason. Angry mobs were reputed for being torch-happy, and as she looked around at the nervous Orses shuffling in their hay it became easy to surrender.

Crossing the yard, Apt presented herself before the leader, looking up. She felt smaller the more she noticed how much bigger the brigands were than her.

"Is this what you're after? Here," Apt yelled with force she didn't feel, flinging her bow towards the leader, who caught it before it touched him. "take it, and go away!"

He rumbled a surprised laugh and issued a command too low for her to hear, riders on either side moving towards her.

"You're coming along." an armored figure growled from beneath its helmet as a spiky-gauntleted arm swooped down to catch her up.

Not as fast as an Orse, in that heavy plate and armor. Probably not as smart either. The Orses were smart, but the brigands were too dumb to use them well. They'd piled in together for intimidation value, but all it would take is one Orse to spook... Apt flashed her hands in front of the mount's eyes and made a significant noise. While the gauntleted fist still caught her on the side of the head, it could not grasp her, and Apt was gratified to see the riders and Orses tumble in on each other like giant lemmings. Apt saw, from the ground where she was laid out, the earth-pounding retreat of galloping hooves.

Apt fell into unconsciousness and dreamed of long ago, knowing that something was happening.

Chapter 5

The something that was happening was a something so sweet Apt wanted to dream this dream forever. She was dreaming of the poet, that his broad, ink-stained fingers were caressing her throbbing head, and where he touched was coolness and relief. He spoke low in the same soothing and safe tones Apt used with injured Orses, touching her brow, her cheek, her lips with gentleness. Apt knew from housemaid's romantic tales that next he would take her in his arms, pressing her against him, declare his love and then...

The poet began to apply a poultice in thick, odorous glops to Apt's face. She sputtered fully awake, for this was no dream. Judging from the smell, maybe a nightmare.

"You're awake." the poet observed, catching Apt's hands as she reflexively moved to rid herself of the horrid paste. "Shh, lie still." Against her better instink, she complied, allowing him to complete his ministrations as, though accompanied by ferocious stench, they also involved him touching her face some more. He layered the goop carefully. As she breathed through her mouth she found that her olfactory senses were pixillating, breaking down, fading away under the surge of information from her skin which was broadcasting useful and fascinating data on the structure of his fingertip whorls, from her eyes that would be publishing the results of their study of his face after their investigation was concluded.

A distant voice in Apt's memory told her it was impolite to stare, and she shut her eyes, allowing touch but still seeing behind her eyelids that face so close seeing her. No, not seeing, but looking at her. Well, not at her, but at the foot-size bolt of pain that had adhered itself somehow to her head. The energy behind the poet's touch and the energy of her own response to it sang the pain lullabies and tucked it lovingly into its nest and stayed with it till it was fast asleep.

There was pleasure to be felt under the sharpening blue eyes and it deepened with the poet's fingertips grasping the point of Apt's chin to turn her head for further attention, the lifting of her fall of hair so that the small hairs on the back of his ungloved wrist whispered to her ears, pleasure in the back of his hand, back-to-back against her nape like dancers of tango who begin their passionate performance by inviting the audience to watch them meet. As the music begins, they are still facing away from each other.

Sometimes the dancers stand distant, as the poet seemed to Apt as he commented on her injury,

"It needs stitches." His composed manner discomposed Apt. With effort she raised herself to regard him where he now stood, running a distressingly curved silver needle through the candle flame.

"Are you a doctor?" Apt asked hopefully. As the poet resumed his seat beside her on the bed (this one not quite so fluffy, much more firm than her first one, and quite comfortable) the poet shook his head, but the warm expression on his face reassured her. Ah, better than a doctor, she thought and then noticed he was pressing her back among the pillows with a strong forearm just the way the housemaids had described.

Would there now be protestations of love? The poet's clear eyes held Apt's now-green gaze.

"This is going to hurt some, I hope you don't mind if I hold you down."

It did hurt, a lot. Luckily, when it was done Apt was left with more memories of the poet's shaking, involuntary breathing (though steady hands) and heat wherever his body leaned on hers that he might attend more closely to his task, than she remembered the puncturing of already-inflamed flesh. The not-fast pull of suture silk threading through, seven times searingly as she watched it up close from her right eye in a blaze of white pain. There was a pull, like a part of Apt's psyche was being drawn up clinging to the strand again and again, layered like a dipped candle, puncturated and knotted with a heart-quivering jerk of thread as if tying her off. It fixed the spiral of her psyche in flesh that would, healed, be stronger than before.

Apt made no sound and didn't struggle until he stood away from her, satisfied with the work, at which point she leapt, surfing on the pain in her head and something else, punching the air with all four limbs and yelling the word she'd studied with Bess. It was amazingly helpful. Apt felt more herself than she had since taking on this new face and told the startled poet how much she appreciated his help, a comment that achieved the reverse of her desired intent, as his open face fell into itself and Apt wondered suddenly if he were old.

He opened jars of unguents and applied them, muttering distractedly,

"I should sooner have come to your aid, especially when I saw what you possessed. But I stayed inside, numb, paralyzed with the others while you faced mounted raiders to defend people you were a stranger to, people who were doing nothing, would do nothing to help you. And that innkeeper..."

"You are doing something now." said Apt. The poet smiled at himself through her, beginning to wind clean white gauze from the bottom of her right cheekbone, over her eye with its neighboring wound. He pulled quite tightly across the left side of Apt's forehead. "Ow. What do you mean, what I possessed?" The poet grimaced apologetically, saying,

"The 'bow' that you hurled so contemptuously at the leader. Oh, the disdain on your face. I would like to think that was why I remained inside...that you were strong enough to defeat them all, and I didn't want to interfere."

"But I wasn't strong enough, and I was hurt."

"You were smart enough to save us all from harm, including yourself, which is better. And if you hadn't been injured..." and here the poet flashed Apt a grin that swooned her, "...I would never have had the pleasure of your acquaintance, nor you of my encyclopedic knowledge of the healing arts."

His smile became rueful, also oreganoful, rosemary and mintful, for his expertise was with the healing herbs of Bess' medicinal garden, he explained, and not extensive whatsoever. A few births with Bess, assisting with the various complaints of the Terrible Boar's staff, a stint as a medic...

"...but I've become distracted." His voice lowered. "Your 'bow'...d'you mean to say that you knew not/the treasure in your keeping?"

"D'you have to say it like that?" Apt sighed.

"How to speak of the
losing of the so long lost,
almost regained and lost again
before mine eyes?"

"I know you're a poet," Apt remarked, "but could you please say it plainly?"

"How could you not know?" cried the poet. "Could you not feel the ancient pow'r, nor, laying hands upon it, hear through your palms the long lost voice of Don Juana Lucia, are you saying that you held the neck of the Harp and felt nothing?" The poet's hands were gripping the sides of his head.

"Nope, it was just a bow." said Apt, to which the poet made a comment that sounded quite a bit like "yaarg". Apt had a bolt of inspiration. "Are there any songs about it?" she inquired sweetly. The poet looked up, head cocked to one side, angst forgotten.

"Oh, many, many, and not just in our language, either. You'll find Harp songs all across this land and in the Far Sea, for that is, of course, whence it came." He paused. "Perhaps," he murmured, eyes dreamy as he reached for his muted black performance harp, "you'd like to hear one?" Apt nodded, not really hearing the poet talk about the history of this piece, who had arranged it for what, simply taking in each deliberate gesture as he took and tuned the instrument, memorizing his preoccupied cobalt eyes as he began to sing.

This is what he sang:

"Hark, all sailors! With woe and grief
To you, I will this most lost of songs
Who are sick at heart, rife with wrongs
To strife and most ill fortunes lief
I will weigh your dolor with one more sad tale
That of Fluisa and the Whale

Born among the currents of the silken deep
They played among the shallows as calf and fry
Till life saw them grown, diving down where ancient sailors lie
To swim through sunken masts of mighty ships asleep
They heard not of the plund'ring of their realms
Nor how were hunted Hornwhales for their helms.

Through the day Fluisa waiting in waters warm
Pearlescent in the deep sea light
Then sought she the Whale all the night
Lit only by the glowing swarm
Of phosphor in the currents above
She swum in search of her immense love

For ivory hunted, fat, for oil and meat
The Hornwhale, tracked without respite
Chased in every hiding place it gained, desp'rate
Until was cut off from all retreat
The last of his kind in the South Sea shone
And in a moment was murdered for flesh and bone.

Fluisa wept rivers unknown to the sea,
T'was all of a wetness most salt and similar
Gathering the few bones left behind by the sailors
She created an implement weeping bitterly
To heal the broken, fill ev'ry lack
Though the Harp's music could not bring him back.

Hark, all sailors! With woe and grief
To you, I will this most lost of songs
Who are sick at heart, rife with wrongs
To strife and most ill fortunes lief
I will weigh your dolor with one more sad tale
That of Fluisa and the Whale"

"That is a sad song." Apt whispered when the last melancholy note had fallen into silence.

"T'is sadder than you know. In some ways, it became sadder after the Harp passed to Don Juana

Lucia, when, after it brought her all the acclaim she could have wished, she withdrew from the world and ordered the Harp destroyed, the pieces scattered."

The poet opened a trunk. Within, a filigreed cube, a skein of shining wires and an ornate pedestal nestled plushly. "I have them now. The voice box, strings and body of the Harp of Don Juana Lucia, attained after awful expense and hardship. To complete the Harp, I have sought its neck, the final part, in all my waking hours, except when I was drunk, or writing." The poet paused, his mouth making a funny line. "It has been my mission to collect and assemble the pieces of the Harp for so long. Terrible it was to see the neck, steps away from me, to see it jammed into a rogue's jerkin, stolen, lost..." he looked into Apt's eye and took her hand, gently supinating it, touched with one fingertip the exposed, chafed palm, "...to hold the hand that held it, that which threw it..." His palm covered hers, he turned her hand, released it, "...and hear you say it was just a bow..."

As the poet's words faded, Apt felt that she was supposed to apologize, but she didn't and was glad to hear the hope in his voice as he told her that even now, two of his friends were hot on the brigand's trail, and he trusted Gies and Essji with this task. "Though I would fain be with them, I am better here with you, to make you better."

The electric shiver still tingling in her palm was almost but not quite enough to distract Apt from the question of why the Antiquarian had released an artifact of such provenance unto her, and with such misinformation! It was perfectly reasonable that she didn't know what it was, but he must have, and for a pathological cataloguer, this was an entirely uncharacteristic act. Was she intended to have this part to play in the Harp's reassembly, or rather in the obstruction of its assembly? She asked this question simply.

"Was it meant to be?"

"Don't get me started on Fate," groaned the poet. "I must regain it, it is the destiny I've chosen."

"But why is it so important for you to do it?" Apt inquired sincerely. The poet stared at her.

"The Harp soothes the human heart, brings peace into the breathing breast and lifts the spirit into Heaven. The bard who played this instrument would be as an angel."

"And famous, too." Apt said, beginning to understand.

"Yes, and rich. Don't forget rich."

*   *   *

The Cat was upset. This often occurred, it is easy enough to irritate felines, but this was getting a bit much. The old man was increasingly uncivil and had of late been refusing to share the meals brought by the monks. These Lattein monks were twice-daily visitors who had in the past merely dropped dinners (that were in themselves a kind of penance, but heavy on the milk, which pleased the Cat mightily) at the door, but they had of late been staying to attempt conversation with the Cat's human. This was an unlikely proposition, the Cat could have told them.

Aside from his normally ferocious intertwining of languages, the man had begun to incorporate random, rapid volume shifts into his speaking voice and adding gestures inappropriate to his subject matter whenever possible. The monks listened, externally calm and interested in the Antiquarian's well-being, but the Cat, watching from the windowsill, began to feel a swelling suspicion, and rising hunger.

Of course the Cat knew the whereabouts of the monastery, which was where food came from, but decided to follow the monks there, sleeking through the grasses beside the path in order to overhear any indiscreet or revealing conversation. Apparently the monks had taken a vow of silence between themselves, for they spoke not at all the long road home.

The Cat was questioning their possible motives to generosity, especially in the face of such ungrateful reception as offered by the old man. Surely any favor the monks believed they owed him had long ago been paid off. After all, they'd been bringing him food twice a day for eleven years.

No, thought the Cat, leaving the unstimulating companions behind with a bolt of turbo feline grace, it would have been twelve years ago, when the great vocalist Don Juana Lucia had stopped singing, and ordered her Harp destroyed. The monks had started coming 'round about that time, the Cat concluded, bouncing up the monastery steps.

* * *

It was late afternoon and the dinner crowd downstairs in the Great Hall of the Open Hart generated a low vibration rising through the timbred walls, the floor and up through the bed, where Apt still lay at the poet's request. Upon his discovery of her lack of address, also of family, or name, he had regarded her quizzically, then let it go, his shrug almost imperceptible. Years in a pub can blunt the sharp tool of inquiry. One might ask, but if the answer is not the one expected, no further interest is indicated, more out of respect for one's own sanity than the other's privacy. He did not offer his own name, for it seemed like flaunting one's riches in front of the poor.

With Apt's assurance that her pain was indeed better but that she would nevertheless stay in bed, the poet responded that he would ensure that one of his friends staying at the inn would check in on her occasionally and that the innkeeper would not, and left to tend to his affairs.

Apt, alone in the golden room, inhaled the scent of his pillow but smelled nothing but the pungent herbs of her bandage.

He returned late, and Apt rose, fairly well, to relinquish his bed.

"No, please rest, of course you must stay. I have the room till tomorrow, and you'll heal better for being in a nice bed."

"It is nice, very firm."

"Isn't it? Some prefer huge downy bedclouds that swallow a body."

"Ugh. Can't roll out of 'em." Apt agreed, informed by her singular experience.

"No purchase. You have excellent taste in beds! Well, I don't even know your name, but at least we know we'd enjoy sleeping together." The poet reddened suddenly. "Not that we'll sleep together, not that I mean that, not at all."

"Why can't we sleep together?" asked Apt, moving to one side of the bed. The poet protested as he sat beside her.

"Dear one, it's not proper, you're ill and in my care. It isn't the honorable thing to do." Apt looked searchingly at the poet's strained expression.

"It would be dishonorable to cause somebody's who's cared for me to sleep on the floor as payment."

"You assume you get the bed? But, seriously lass, t'wouldn't be decent."

"Well, if you want to sleep indecently, you can, but I'm wearing my clothes to bed. We'll sleep like Orses."

"Standing up?"

"Better not." she grinned.

The poet lay closely next to Apt in the perfectly firm but narrow bed. She was not sleeping and occasionally the unbandaged part of her face would contract as though the pain had surprised her but she was uncomplaining, her flanks and deep breaths pressing against him as though to instruct him in the behavior of resting Orses. He thought he began to have an idea of what she meant. As she relaxed further, her head turned, causing a shiver of discomfort. The poet whispered,

"Is there aught I can do, lassie?" She began to shake her head then thought better of it.

"There's more insult to this than ache. I've been kicked and stepped on by Orses...accidentally of course, they meant nothing by it, and I've fallen every so often. But it seems to me there's some poison in a blow to the face that will take longer to heal than the wound itself."

The poet shifted himself so that he was face to face with the tender and wise young woman in his bed. "It is a bitter poison," he agreed. "If you wish it, I have one remedy in my pharmacopeia that is a sovereign antidote for this kind of venom." She replied with expressive eyes, and the poet leant close to apply the cure.

In the morning, Apt awoke with little pain and turned to commend the poet on the efficacy of his treatment, but he had departed, and she would have thought it all just a dream save for the bruise-colored tulips, tied with a lace from the poet's shirt, that lay on the pillow beside her.

Chapter 6

A knock came at the door and it opened to reveal one of the flowerly ladies who had grouped around the poet after his performances. Apt, still half-asleep, was startled by the figure formed of careful bulges and drapes of teal, turquoise and cloth-of-gold brocade with matching hat and dancing slippers that seemed veritably too bright, and worse, with a vociferously cheery demeanor to match.

Oh dear, thought Apt, will she play nursemaid and say how are we then and overflow with vaguely comforting phrases?

Yes. Elbu was here at the poet's behest, to look in on Apt AGAIN, she'd done so previously, but the patient had been dead to the world. According to Elbu, Apt looked a sight, a remark whose redundancy and unveiled criticism did not improve the looks of the observation's subject one whit. Elbu prattled, refusing to sit.

"and then can you imagine my face, it just fell, the other ladies told me, when He approached me--as He often does, you know, seek me out, for inspiration in his Work--and told me, hahahahaha, that He had a young woman in His room, a YOUNG WOMAN can you credit it well I never so of course you know I can deny Him nothing hahahahaha so agreed readily because it

64

was obvious He was sporting with me--He does make me a bit of a favorite--and I admit I was a teensy bit miffed when I discovered He"

Elbu inhaled

"was in earnest and that He truly did have another woman in His chambers and it was dreadful how upset it made me I was quite overwrought as I climbed the stairs to minister to you imagining well you know how it is, all the dire thoughts of your true love in the arms of another beautiful woman?" She paused in a way that almost suggested that she was awaiting a response, but it was merely to begin speaking again with renewed vigor and levity, as though mocking her own fears,

"of course not I need say no more of it but of course you can imagine my relief upon seeing you hahahahaha and so I said to myself hahahahaha Elbu, you are such a silly, in His warm-hearted way He has taken this dirty, scabrous waif into His care I do quite love that about Him, don't you, the way He is so impetuously GOOD oh I quite adore it, it's ravishing how His noble impulses inspire one to selfless service is it not?"

That misleadingly inviting pause.

"And selfless it is I assure you for I myself am petrified of the sight of b-l-o-o-d you see I can't even bear the sound of the word but He has asked me to change your bandage and I will conquer my own delicacy to do what He has asked of me I will endeavor to look away as much as possible but I may faint remind me to give you some smelling salts to wave under my nose in that event but He also said something about a jar of unguent and I don't know which one He meant." She stopped abruptly, viewing the collection of bottles perplexedly. It was a tableau until Apt realized that Elbu had stopped talking and was actually waiting for a reply. She seized the opportunity.

"Please, don't trouble yourself on my account! A lady of your delicacy should not be expected to risk her constitution performing a task that I can do myself." Elbu brightened for a moment then dulled, aluminummy resolve in her expression.

"No no I can do it you'll see which jar was it?"

"Did he say what it had in it?"

"Well it was all quite exciting, what with the everything, and He was giving me all of these complicated instructions He chose me because He could feel my own healing powers most sensitive people can detect them they are ever so powerful I was selected to be apprenticed to a great teacher in the arcane arts and it has been my heart's desire secondary of course to my love to bring these mystic secrets to the world so I am the natural choice for this mission distasteful as it is oh yes now I remember because it had such an ugly name coltsfoot who would want to put that on themselves really"

"It's the one over there in the green glass container." Apt said icily.

"Aren't you the clever one however did you know that?

"They're labeled."

"Oh, you read, what a pleasant conceit." She fetched the jar and seated herself gingerly on the bed's very edge as far away from Apt as possible. "I'm ready, once more into the fray and all that. He did ask ME to do it and I want to be able to report on my bravery if, er, when He asks so we'll just splash some medicine on that naughty scrape jolly good show with the mob by the way I certainly wouldn't have done it like that but different strokes as they say and we'll wrap your sad little head up spic and span in a nice bandage you'll see how courageous I am the depths I will sink to I am committed."

"There are seven bloody black stitches with bits sticking out like spider's legs." Apt said agreeably. "And maybe pus." The jar, dropping from Elbu's be-ringed hand seemed to hit the floor after the door had slammed shut behind the rest of her.

The jar of Tussilago farfara hadn't broken (it had been dropped from numb fingers, not flung in horror), so Apt made use of the supplies to treat herself with the mossy-smelling tincture and change the bandage, which calm process did nothing to subdue the inner seething fractalling within Apt as a result of Elbu's horrendous bedside manner. As she left the room behind and descended the stair, wriggling masses of responses to Elbu's outrageous speech were trying to be said (a chess game of permutations and all of them stone-stopping the harping, carping Elbu in her tracks) when, all of a sudden, Apt heard a hiss. She halted on the step, midway on the flight.

There was nobody nearby; the inn was quiet as most everyone was at a funeral or two. The hiss came again. Apt felt impatient.

"What! Quit hissing."

The esprit de l'escalier was leaning against a newel post, casually examining his very sharp fingernails. He explained his occupation to her,

"Je vais vers ceux qui ont besoin de moi, lorsqu'ils ont besoin de dire ce qui ne doit être entendu et lorsque tout est devenu regret." and Apt was more than happy that she had been in on the Antiquarian's French mode, as it was clearly sensible to avail herself of the esprit's services.

She began to vent. When she had exhausted her writhing mass of angry response, the esprit came up with a few real zingers that were so mean they made Apt laugh, which she did for a while as the esprit returned to his slightly-stained fingernails. Apt descended the staircase much relieved.

It occurred to her that now she was alone she could just change her whole head again as the folio was still in her possession. Then, recalling the intense discomfort of her previous attempts and considering how it might prove a challenge to maintaining intimacy with the poet if her face was different from the one he'd met her in, Apt resolved to enjoy the anonymity and privacy that simply appearing hurt (which she was) or in need of help (not so much) would offer her as she passed through the town of Bonhomie, whose inhabitants, as Apt had already witnessed, made themselves scarce when somebody was in trouble. Her theory was sound: Apt found she was largely invisible.

She was travelling light, having given her seven arrows away to the giant and now, bearing only the folio, an extra pair of socks and a single tulip petal, Apt remembered that Bonhomie was a seaside town.

*　　*　　*

What of the Cat? It were a bluish shadow against the dim walls, occupying its time in peaceful misadventure until dinner. The abbey's cavernous kitchens had some ideal spyholes for an agile Cat, and it was not long before its patient pale green eye observed a cook deposit the dinner (Tonight! Coagulous Ooze!) into a familiar carrying container, which was retrieved by two monks. The Cat, in the darkness around their skirts, moved soft as dust.

*   *   *

The poet, Rex, was at this time celebrating with Gies and Essji, who had returned triumphant with the 'bow' in hand. He had ridden out far to meet them, and knew by their riding as they approached that all had gone well (which could have been surprising considering the odds of two against seven, unless one were acquainted with the twins). They were both wide men, also long, and a bit thick, but with stout hearts, raised well by a mamma who had not been expecting either the financial or physical impact of having twins, and when asked after delivery how she was feeling, replied "Sorely Grave and Gravely Sore." They became G.S. and S.G.

Essji, or Sorely, was mostly the surlier of the two, born a full three minutes ahead of the dismally distempered Gravely. Both were music lovers and while they also fought, they could not be called fighters as the word implied a level of organization that was not in their skillset. Neither of these friends of the poet was amiable by any social measure, however the three of them got on well and had some marvelous adventures. This had definitely been one of those and they relished the telling of it, with much pounding of fists on tabletop and in air, occasional demonstrative kicks and some sound effects that had the first few customers of the Open Hart's evening rush either looking agitatedly in their direction, or, like the innkeeper, pointedly ignoring the "aaaarrrghs" and brandishings of rather enormous examples of weaponry that accompanied the seamless flow of the story as told by the excited, momentarily happy twins.

"And then we lopped it off, so t'were messy but it"
"worked like a mind bomb and they"

"as much as wrapped it in pretty paper to give to us"

"like a birthday present, so"

"happy birthday to you, Rexy." and with that, Gies handed the Harp's neck to the poet below the cover of the table, and the poet's hands touched his life's dream. He circumspectly placed it among the Harp's other components in their case. A faint, astral hum could instantly be heard, and the poet shut the case quickly.

Their celebration lasted late into the night, and it was only upon returning to his room that the poet drunkenly remembered the female and wondered if she would still be there, if she was better or worse, how she had liked his cure. The room was bare of nameless Orsers and Rex could not decide what that meant to him, if anything.

*   *   *

Probably t'was the purple powder that pickled the professor's provisions, permitted the puss, passing precisely past prelates and portraits picturing pontiffs, perusing for possible portals, pacing precipitously because the Cat really had to p.

When it saw the front door, it was a blur to the bush.

*   *   *

Apt was 15/16ths basking in the sun, she didn't want to remove the bandage and get sand in herself. Baking, blissing, basking in the aftermath of having seen the sea, walked in the waves, discovered the shells and what sand does, the sounds of the busy beach, barkers and buskers, had done her wonders. She had eaten ice cream and a nap beckoned.

Suddenly a shocked nasal voice from under the umbrella on Apt's left demanded,

"What is that horrid smell?"

Apt thought of the Cat, what it had said about humans. I wonder if it's me? She smelled fine, unless the reeking horrible stench of the sea was actually her...oh, the bandage. She removed herself, much to the Nose's gratification, to a small secluded inlet, where she unwound the heated, sticky gauze.

The bandage's contents beggared description, Apt had seen some fairly gross stuff but this was visceral, or whatever the equivalent was with a head wound. She squooshily wadded up the bandage and cast it as far out into the sea as she could, which didn't seem near far enough, and washed the wound in stinging salt water. It felt better without the wrappings, allowed to breathe clean air and dry in the sun.

Finally settling into that nap, head on a log and feet in the water, she felt a baleful flick on her great toe. She opened one eye to see, majestically command-ing and hypnotic even in a semi-beached position, an Undine.

"I am literally sick of humans throwing your crap in the water because it disgusts you too much to look at it. It's your crap!" The Undine heaved the sodden mess of encrusted gauze onto Apt's legs, which Apt reflex-ively withdrew, apparently to the Undine's plan, for in her moment of imbalance, Apt was seized by the hand. Breaching, the Undine rolled Apt into the crashing sea and jetted with her into the depths, far and fast.

Chapter 7

*I*n the poet's room at the Open Hart were convened himself, Gies and Essji. Also assembled, but not yet fully complete, was the Harp. It hummed softly, pulsing graciously upon a table.

"More beautiful than I could have imagined." the poet whispered, loving with his eyes the ancient instrument before him. "You can hardly tell it's missing a string. I'll just avoid playing 'The Lark's Happy Song' or Halmer's Exceptionally Trebulous Classics, especially No. 4, and it won't mean a thing that it ain't got that string."

"Doo-wop doo-wop doo-wop doo-wop doo-wop doo-wop doo-wop doo-ahhh." sang the twins obligingly. As the poet took the Harp from the table and positioned it to play, a hush descended in anticipation of the Harp's exquisite voice being heard for the first time in a dozen years.

*   *   *

Underwater with the Undine there was no time to think, all was feeling, squidding through the strata of colours in a cold cold hot explosion of water. The Undine held Apt so tightly the last gulp of air had long ago departed from her lungs and she could sense her cells popping, one by one until finally the Undine slowed. Apt tucked securely under one winglike arm, the Undine blew a large bubble into her webbed, lacy hand and somehow inserted Apt into it, whereupon the Undine scrutinized her abductee closely. With the bubble on and oxygen coursing into her blood, Apt was able to scrutinize back.

An Undine was not the same as a mermaid, which disappointed Apt somewhat, as she had pictured the embodiment of her favorite word as a lovely female, long hair flowing around her mostly human body and iridescent fishtail, perhaps with seashells as a brassiere. The real thing was more like an armed dolphin with a shark's dorsal fin, larger than Apt and bearing a face that was decidedly fishy, noseless, lipless (though festooned with wiggly catfish barbels), an eye on either side of the head. There was no clamshell lingerie. There was nothing for a clamshell to linger on. The tubular, scaled form was sleek and built for fast speed, which it resumed now that Apt was oxygenated.

Those who have seen underwater nature know the indescribable visions that met Apt's terrestrial eyes; the spiraling shoals of silver fishes moving with a single thought, frondy sea pens and mysterious reefs whose inhabitants peered out curiously as the pair passed, a few creatures that looked as though some fish god in their origin story had become overly enthusiastic and kept adding ornamentation well past the point of functionality.

A single octopus jetted alongside them for awhile, in subliminal and polychromatic conversation with the Undine as they streaked through the deep, clear green. The wonders of this new realm struck Apt with the thought that there was as much to learn about the world below the waves as of the world above, and she hoped that she would be allowed to see more of the sights.

That the Undine had not brought Apt here as a tourist was clear when they came to their destination, a vast effulgent dump, burning like zirconium at the bottom of a cavern that stretched as far as the eye could see. Everything from carriages to enormous drums of waste, some exhaling brilliantly poison-frog-green effluent, had been assembled here by the undersea dwellers.

The contrast between the beauty of the aqueous world and the obviously human-generated garbage heap was painful. The Undine looked sternly at Apt as if to say, "there, you see what you've done?" as Apt regarded her species' profligacy. She wanted to say that she had never seen the sea before today, and was innocent of this crime, but she was forced to recall all the times she'd chucked muck from the stables into the convenient river near the big house and could not protest her innocence. The water in the dumping trench was cancerous and cloudy. Though mostly trapped by the cavern walls, it was apparent that the poisons were not stable and that the purity of the surrounding waters was being contaminated day after day.

Apt wished for speech to apologize, and tried to let her eyes express what her voice could not, looking entreatingly into one of the Undine's eyes. The sea creature seemed to understand, and with a push of her silvery, muscular tail, rose with Apt from the sea floor up through the crushing depths.

Apt's bubble popped on collision with the air. She bobbed in the waves, grateful to feel the wind on her face, and turned to the Undine. Despite her sympathy and sorrow for the sights she'd seen, her enlightened self-interest informed her that she was far out to sea and she'd be well-advised to cannily negotiate a land-deal with the irked creature. The Undine regarded Apt with hard humor and said,

"If we returned to earth all the garbage that's been dumped in the water over the years, your kind would be swimming in muck. The sewage alone...ha! You think that the sea is just a large waste bin, some of your fisher folk," and here she muttered a flowery curse and spat, "even go so far as to call it "the chuck", as in "chuck it in the sea". It's abominable."

"You're right," Apt agreed. One eye evaluated her coolly.

"Agreeing doesn't make it better, leg walker."

"I know."

"What will you do about it?" the Undine demanded. Apt looked around at the limitless ocean.

"Well, if you abandon me here, I can do nothing, for I will certainly drown and become just one more piece of trash on your floor."

"Oh, we don't mind the bodies, there's good meat on a sailor and the bones can be useful for coral." Apt didn't like the way this was going, and thought flattery might help.

"Undine is my favorite word, you are so fortunate to have such a beautiful name."

"I am not called Undine." the Un-Undine retorted. "Leg walkers call me that because in their pretty pictures I undulate. Did you see me undulating?" Apt remembered the creature's torpedo power, her blurring, arrow-flight speed.

"Absolutely not." Apt replied promptly.

"I am called Anenome. A more precise name, meaning wind flower, as I flow like the wind." Apt withheld her knowledge that anenomes were also small red and purple blossoms, correctly assuming that arguing on the subject of identity was not the best way to get herself safely to shore. "I also share that name with the little stayput waving beings below," continued the

Undine affably, "it's such a good name, more than one of us can have it. Do you have a name?"

"So far, Apt, Lassie and Leg Walker, but I doubt any of them are my true name."

"Apt is a good rhyming name."

"So they say."

Apt's amiable nature had mollified Anenome. The creature offered to return her to land, if in turn Apt would spread the word about the grave misuse to which humans were putting the sea. Apt promised she would. The creature bore her gently among the waves, ignoring the seagulls' mockery, until they reached a sandy shore where Apt was deposited. The Un-Undine assured her of the likelihood of human habitation and reminded Apt of her promise before arching back into the sea.

*   *   *

The Cat had single-pawedly unveiled the plot of the Lattein monks. After its relieving trip to the bush, the Cat had returned to the abbey's still-room for a close investigation of the violet dust that had been shaken into the old man's meal. Up close, taking care not to inhale too deeply of the memory-bane, the Cat could smell confusion, suspicion and forgetfulness. The Cat knew from lying on top of the man's studies (while the man was trying to read them) that this exotic concoction had been discovered in the Ades when an enemy had used it to obscure and blur the recollections of Aders who had stumbled upon something significant.

The Aders had returned from their discovery with no remembrance of it, and with a hefty dose of aggression besides, which occurrence had been chronicled by their squire. The only symptom of the memory-bane's poisonous nature was found in the quantities of purple phlegm expectorated by the Aders, which was analyzed to identify a mineral and herbal composite which was then painstakingly reproduced by the Lattein monks.

The most useful aspect of this drug was that the one afflicted had no notion that they were, and often risked being considered mad by others. The monks called it Obscurata and it had found application among members of the order who wished to leave to return to secular life without compromising the cloistered secrets of the monastery.

The fact that the old man was being dosed with such long-term regularity suggested to the Cat that he knew something the monks considered better unknown. The Cat, of course, knew exactly what this was, but no one thought to ask.

With feline inspiration and much effort the Cat dragged the container outside, dug a hole and upended it so that the grains poured out, then collected some dried grape pomace from an empty barrel in the still-room and refilled the vial with the similarly-colored stuff. The Cat would just have to hope that the dispensing monks avoided inhaling, for it smelled quite different, though both memory-bane and wine can share properties inducing forgetfulness and belligerence. Although its mission was accomplished, the Cat journeyed home still far from satisfied.

*   *   *

Making her way inland, pletely at a loss as to her whereabouts, Apt saw that she was at the outskirts of a city. A large banner welcomed her to the Land of Com. This aided little in her prehension, for the Antiquarian had never mentioned this place, not even in myth. Could it be she was discovering a new world unknown to the pendium of knowledge possessed by the widely-travelled Antiquarian? Thrilled, Apt gazed wide-eyed at the metropolis around and above her where impossibly tall buildings crowded the sky, seeming to lean over the thronged streets. There was an awful lot to see of peoples, conveyances, animals and more to hear. Though the language was English, Apt found it unintelligible, so she, undirected, took a less-crowded path which led to a tremendous confection of a building where trains rolled in and out among puffs of steam and screeching wheels.

Standing still in utter confusion as tides of travelers recalled to Apt the way schools of fish had moved in the crystal ocean, she felt a bit at sea.

"You seem lost." a friendly voice mented.

"Also a bit damp." said another. Apt inclined her head to the two fellows before her.

"Both, thanks for noticing. What land is this?"

"This is the Land of Com."

"I think I may need some directions." she smiled. The two men introduced themselves to Apt as the great friends Rade Patriot and Rade Padre, (Com was a Munist country) and were helpful with their suggestions.

"North-by-north-left is good, so is Through." But Rade Padre was convinced that because this was the third of the third of the third, that Orange-by-right-hook was a better direction unless the visitor was unequipped for a Bat Zone, in which case she could Bear Down or, if preferred, Bear Up. These were all good directions, they asserted.

"Very nice directions," Apt exercised diplomacy. "may I ask which direction you are going?"

"We are going in the 974th direction." Rade Patriot replied. "I would be happy to tell you the ones in between as it is a special interest of mine, but Rade Padre and I are muting to work and our train is ing, so we must be off."

"Perhaps our visitor would like to acpany us?" Rade Padre inquired. Apt accepted eagerly. The men provided her a ticket with their pliments and all boarded the train.

Though the route was scenic, it flashed by much faster than it would if it were seen from the back of an Orse, and Apt felt dizzy. The Rades sensed her disposure and sought to fort her with their poems and positions, for though they worked in the Puter Division full-time, they were nonetheless both well-rounded sorts with a healthy appreciation for the arts. Apt refrained from menting that their poems were mostly inprehensible to her and did little to assuage her queasiness.

Suddenly, the train's inter announced an emergency. Amid the great motion, the Rades led Apt to the space between two cars to see if they could determine the source of threat. The train was stalled on a bridge over a broad lake set in dense forest, tops of the trees seen below the trestle. Apt turned to ask the Rades if they knew what was going on, but the answer was both self-evident and unheard as the train lurched horribly. Apt pitched backwards (483rd direction) from the train and could see the disfiture in the Rades' diminishing faces as she dropped past blurring trees into the lake below.

*   *   *

It is better to not describe the sound produced by the poet's first stroke of the Harp, for if one were to call it, say, atonal, then one would have to mark the word atonal in the dictionary "Exhausted, Do Not Use." The poet removed the blanket he had thrown over the Harp to shut it up and gazed bewilderedly at it as though it had become a slavering monster. An angry voice at the door demanded to know what was going on. Concealing the Harp, the poet opened the door to the florid innkeeper, who shouted,

"What was that awful din?"

"What din?" the poet asked sweetly. The innkeeper noticed the hulking twins in matching hear-no-evil poses and wheeled on the poet.

"Don't you play dumb with me, what do you have to say about it?"

The poet slipped some coins into the innkeeper's hand.

"Say about three silver pieces?"

After the innkeeper left, the poet resumed his gloomy contemplation of the Harp. He needed that string. Obviously, he would try it with his own more secular harp strings, far away from other humans, with cotton batting, but he had a hunch that the Harp could not be satisfied by a common string and that the best he could hope for would be that the Harp did not explode in outrage. How to find the true string? Maybe the lass still had it, had used it for a necklace or to tie up her hair.

Maybe it was where he had found the others, deep in a catacomb. A few years back, the poet had received guidance that the strings of the Harp would be found in the burial shelf of a veteran Ader, the M.V.V. Saaf Dutch. He had died here at home and had been provided full military funeral honors in the catacombs, so it was fairly easy for the poet to find the veteran's shelf hung with tapestry, weapons and a dusty flag. The poet had searched the shelf carefully, probing among M.V.V. Dutch's belongings and the enshrouded remains of M.V.V. Dutch until he touched what he hoped was a bundle of strings. It was, and he thought he'd taken them all, but they were very fine, and he could have missed one.

"What'll we do? All that work for nothing." Gies sulked, hunkered over himself like an overhanging cliff. Essji was pacing tensely in the small space. The poet plopped himself on the bed and gazed out the window at scudding clouds, then said they would have to continue their search and asked the twins to return to the catacombs. Gies moaned reproachfully, Essji just stalked heavier.

"Now you'll have to go (right march to the bedstead) off looking for (left march to the window) some nameless wench and us in the smelly old crypts, digging (right march to the bedstead with a stop by the table for refreshment) through dusty mummies for (paused dramatically at the foot of the bed where the poet reclined, picking his teeth with a stick, barely listening) an invisible ferding thread." Essji complained. "And how d'you think you'll find the girl, poet?" he challenged.

The poet, seeming to be on the far side of his own disappointment, confidence returning moment by moment, inclined a lazy head in Essji's direction.

"I always do," he grinned. He was not entirely unhappy that his quest had been extended. Swinging his legs off the bed, he sat up right sharp, regarding his loyal companions. "and I'll find this one too, I warrant. Gentlemen, our search continues and though the way be hard, by my faith the Harp will sing again!"

*   *   *

Apt, unhurt, though perhaps having had enough of being violently immersed in liquid for the time being, had travelled beyond the borders of Com and had not yet entered the Land of Con, as evinced by her complete confidence. She swam slowly to the silky-sanded shore through fresh water. This was definitely a turn for the better, she mused, surveying the inviting landscape and selecting a site for shelter on the lightly-treed lakeshore.

For many weeks she enjoyed improving her shelter in the mornings, then relaxing under the dappling sun of afternoon listening to the gentle lake lap, and in

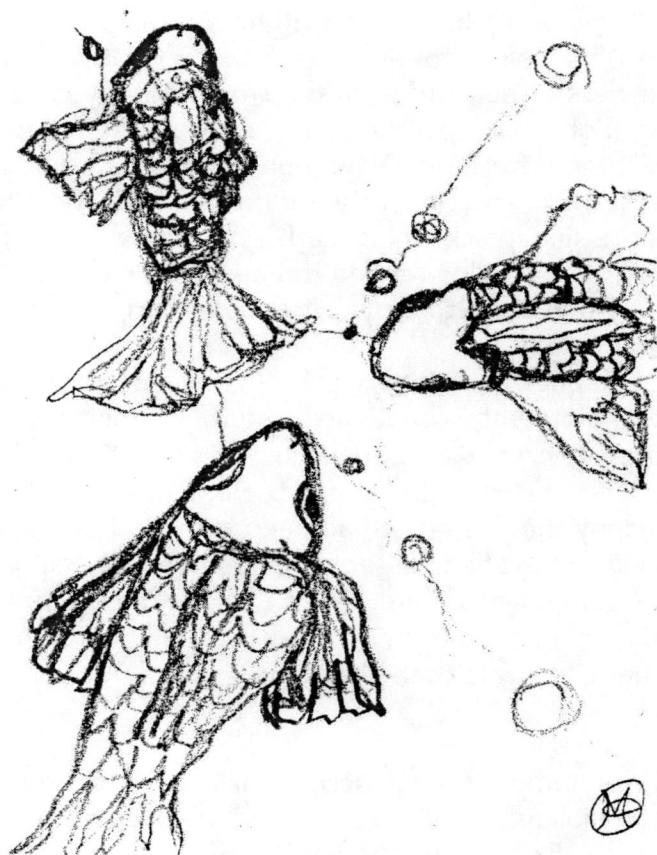

the evenings apologetically (thinking of Anenome) but savouringly dining on trout with sweetroot and berries, which were plentiful. Apt had caught the first trout by practical application of one of the Antiquarian's tales of the natural world.

Finding a warm shallow and several shining fish snoozing there, she thought to try her hand at tickling trout and approached them very slowly. She chose one who appeared to be especially lazy, and stroked its belly with one finger.

The trout began to giggle, miniscule bubbles of sound breaking on the water's surface. Apt wiggled her finger and the fish laughed uncontrollably, shaken soda froth now churning with silvery mirth so that Apt could hardly see the fish. The laughter was contagious, and Apt could hardly stop laughing as she scooped the contorted trout from the water and dashed its head on a stone. Though that, her first self-provided meal, had been very tasty, the next time she used a slender plait of willow and bait. It seemed inappropriate to eat somebody with whom one had laughed so long.

One could say the days passed uneventfully, but that would be incorrect, for there were very many events every day among the fish, the dragonflies and lakeskippers, ravens, ducks and owls and once, a bear. It was a busy and pleasant life, a welcome change from the violent chaos that had preceded it, and Apt felt she could probably continue this way forever if not for the promises she had made, almost without intending to, that increasingly demanded her return to the world.

She'd promised the Cat she'd try to find something to help the Antiquarian, promised the Antiquarian she'd return his property (which she still possessed, waterlogged but legible), promised the monk of the rose and lily any information or remedy that might help Lentdemain, and promised Anenome she would try to get the humans to stop dumping crap in the water.

It was a pretty full agenda, and idyllic as the home she'd created here was, she had things to do. It was, however, easy to put off doing them while still in the warmer part of autumn, while the sun still shone so well and the berries still ripened and it appeared like such a tremendous amount of work was required even to begin the journey, not to mention she'd have to do something about her personal presentation. Page 12 of the folio could help with the clothing, but she hadn't seen anything in there about hair.

One rainy day, Apt was unsuccessfully fishing in the shelter under the bridge when she noticed a tiny figure far above her in the grey mist, lowering itself slowly down an impossibly long rope whose end rippled the gloomy lake's face with the climber's efforts.

Apt decided her visitor's arrival would be a while yet, so went back to her cottage to fetch some sweet-root scones and a woven birch waterbasket of herbal tea. She laid them out on a decorated deer-hide (her first and only deer, and a sad story she would prefer not to recall) on the dry sand below the bridge and squinted at the figure that was now almost descended. It was the poet.

Chapter 8

*S*o like himself, he chose to take the last twenty feet of the journey in a daring dive, swimming below the surface almost to the spot where Apt sat, with tea steaming in an earthenware cup awaiting him. He took her rough hand in his two wet ones.

"I found you!" he whispered incredulously. She passed him the tea, breathing deeply to help control her shaking.

"There's only one cup, we'll have to share." said Apt, half-hoping he would enquire after the cup's provenance, for Apt was very proud of the underground kiln she'd built to fire tiles and dishes made from local greenish clay. The dishes had come out especially well though she, not expecting company, had only made one of each kind. The poet set the carefully patterned cup aside without looking at it, for his eyes were fixed on her own.

Apt wondered what he was seeing, and felt something unfamiliar. The Orses had never cared what she looked like, she always smelled fine and that was the important thing. She'd never sought attention by the various arts employed by the housemaids of paints, stays and unpleasant regimens for the hair, and had selected her present face only as it was sufficiently different from her previous one, with no thought to improvement (though she did think her eyes were quite nice). As such she was unacquainted with the nervous whisper along her spine telling her that she was probably the least appealing person the poet had ever seen.

Apt attempted to quell her raging insecurity with the knowledge that function was always more important than form (and you can't build a cottage without breaking a few fingernails) but she still felt a dread contrast between the lake creature she'd become and the poet's handsome, though sodden, good looks. However, his warm blue gaze admitted none of Apt's irrational fears. The pleasure in his eyes seemed to praise her, untangle her hair, wash her face and dress her in silk as he said formally,

"I have long searched for you, through unknown and dangerous lands."

"Yes, how did you find me? I'd've thought my trail was cold."

"Yes, and wet. It didn't take long to track you to the beach near the Open Hart, and many people remembered your bandaged head, but t'was many days 'til was found the one child had seen you abducted by a monster that came out of the ocean. So I waited by the shore and there I met the Undine."

"She's not an..."

"Not a monster, I knew it, though with monstrous strength she was heaving a large chesterfield, quite water-damaged, onto the beach. Peculiar habit that, perhaps having to do with the mating season. Thinking you might have taken ship, I asked if she had seen you among any of the boats' passengers and she replied you'd been her passenger. When I told her I was seeking you, she asked me my purpose and what I told her convinced her to carry me here safely."

"What did you say?" Apt's whisper moved like dry leaves in slight wind.

"Well, I told her t'was true love."

"Did you."

"Aye."

"Is that why you came for me? True love?" The poet reddened under Apt's direct gaze.

"Love of a sort, anyway. I really just need to ask you a question."

The poet told her of the recovery of the Harp's neck, its reassembly and the unfortunate result. "Losing that one string makes more of a difference than I could have known. I've come to ask you if you know its location."

"No." said Apt. The poet was crestfallen.

At that moment, a trio of soldiers appeared from the woods near the bridge's foundation. They offered Apt and the poet their dolences, for in the day's tretemps in the recent war between Com and Con, trol of these lands had been ceded to the Con's rule, and Apt and the poet would need to clude their stay in these parts. Not daring to tradict the soldier's decree which seemed introvertible, the pair tracted to catch the next necting train at the nearby station.

The soldiers being vivial fellows, they allowed Apt and the poet to stop by the cottage so that Apt could collect her few things while the poet looked around in astonishment at the cozy little house. As she left it behind, hoping the soldiers would not be too hard on the home she had come to love, Apt soled herself that she was leaving with the poet, and that love "of a sort" was possibly better than any number of trout.

At the station, which was much closer than Apt had expected, so complete had been her seclusion, the Ductor punched their tickets with an askance glance at her muddy person. Apt resolved to make a certed effort to clean up in the train's restroom.

87

By the time she returned to their seats, the train had crossed the border into Po, so Apt confronted the et, demanding to know more about the Harp's wers. The hour growing late, he briefly described the legendary quality of the Harp's voice, that it was so very lovely as to bring a soul back from the brink of death or madness and that the great singer Dona Juana Lucia had ordered it destroyed when she stopped performing.

"Why did she stop, if she was so great?"

"Sometimes, great is too good. Her contemraries reported that before her disappearance, she was so besieged with admirers that a security team specialized in bouquet control had to be added to her entourage. She was in demand everywhere she went, which at first had been her goal but later in her career was a curse, and she blamed in large part the Harp for bringing her such fortune.

"No one knows where she went, but it was common knowledge among musicians when it happened that she had left a note which said that she had broken the Harp, and strewn its pieces and herself, and that she hoped none of them would ever be found. Many searched, but I knew they would not succeed. I knew I would be the one to find the Harp and make my name, for I did not believe that her fame had been such a great burden, and though I was but a child, my quest was begun."

The et's noble head was framed against the train's dark window like a rtrait on velvet, soulful eyes revisiting his innocent child-self.

"Did you have help?" Apt asked, seeing before her the young boy's ignant longing, and the seeming imssiblity of its fulfillment.

"Yes." Said the et, shortly, and changed the subject. He said the luggage rter had told him the dining car was featuring ached salmon and lenta and the gaming car was offering roulette, ker and other amusements. The et recommended that even if Apt wasn't hungry they should seek some tables and lite diversions. The night was passed in queer games and an uncomfortable sleep as the train sped on, crossing the border into De.

This stination had been cided on by the poet (with manly termination) on the grounds that this caying city was the home of two sistaz who might have turned up something in their own work on the poet's behalf. It was also a port, with frequent partures to Bonhomie, to facilitate the next step of the poet's plan.

Mentia and Lirium were two elders who received the poet and Apt gladly, Lirium especially gladly, as she perceived the visitors to be dignitaries from one of her previous lives in Ka, that had brought many rich gifts at which Lirium marveled. While her sista praised the treasures (*"O such Lapis, the golden sky on the midnight stars did doth illumine --illuminium--illuminum--illuminatum--what a lovely brooch. Platinum? Platinarum--platinatus—planetarium~ "*), Mentia welcomed the poet and Apt into their home. The poet clared his intention to make tea and headed for the kitchen.

On the cab ride from the station to the sistaz' crepit town home, the poet had explained to Apt that they were the true finders of the Harp's pieces. They spent much time in Sane, where the poet as a youth had met them while going through a teen time and they had first taken a fondness to him. It was a meeting place for many of the world's dreamers and easy to get to, especially for those who dreamed while awake.

The most popular club in Sane was the Subconscious, and multitudes thronged there nightly. Privacy was unknown and the secret thoughts of many were on display. The sisters ensured that any mention, thought, dream or desire of anything that might even possibly be a part of the broken Harp was reported to the poet. It was only their oracular transmissions that had led him to the far-flung pieces, and he wished voutly as he cautiously compiled tea in the sistaz' unstable kitchen (though rife with peril, this was still more prudent than having Mentia make the tea) that their wisdom and madness would aid his course once more.

Though they were still helpfully inclined towards him, they had no new information. Perhaps if they were to revisit Don Juana Lucia's summer palace in Sane, abandoned these twelve years past, the poet might find something previously overlooked. This at least was the precis of a conversation that took three hours and four pots of tea.

The sistaz' coach drove them in Sane, and dropped them off at a massive door, which had been made fast with a padlocked chain. Delirium took the chain in her hands, and began to shake it vigorously. There was a crack, and the lock fell away in pieces.

"Tremens, a little talent I have." Delirium said modestly.

Reverently, they entered the palace. Though long-stripped of any valuable or remotely movable object, and looking as though usually inhabited by large messy mice with a working knowledge of spray cans, the grandeur of the mansion's arching design was proof enough that here had once dwelt a person of stature, and the merest whisper, susurrating to the vaulted glass ceiling and resonating in the ear, suggested to the listener that the power of the occupant's voice had shaped the very walls.

Deliberately, but already expecting that their search would prove futile, the four investigated the mansion. Perusing an enormous, dusty manor in search of a single thread was enough to keep the foursome founded squarely in Sane as both methodically and erratically they scanned each of the rooms.

Hours into it, Dementia opened a door at the top of a narrow stair and thought she saw a light on in a room at the end of a hall lined with suits of armor. The others checked and she was right, but as Dementia could often be a bit indiscreet, Delirium offered to wait with her here while the poet and Apt made their way quietly down the corridor, past the ranks of empty men.

* * *

Bish O'Prick was crazy with impatience, so had gone in Sane. There he had heard through the grapevine (a great amplifying device for the tiny voice of the local guidebug) that the poet had returned. O'Prick next sought out a flighty gossip, hovering with a gabble of others at a feeder suspended from nothing. The brash bird could not resist informing him that the poet and the ruffled person were visiting one of the gossip's favorite topics of conversation, the sistaz (or, as the bird preferred to call them, "THOSE women").

The man laughed unpleasantly, knowing that the sistaz would keep Rex for a long while over tea and biscuits, but that he, not trusting the thoroughness of previous searches, would eventually come to the summer palace. O'Prick, however, would get there first. Reports had come to him from a villainous innkeeper in Bonhomie of the poet's complicity in a certain terrible noise, and Bish suspected what that noise had been. He could feel that his quest for the Harp was very close to its conclusion.

Now, waiting to be discovered, Bish once again remembered how he had come to the Harp, back when he had been the Bishop Rick, novice spiritual leader of a company in the fourth Ade. It was there he had met Pol, a seasoned campaigner, and a fiery beauty named Lucia, who was mostly there to fly in the face of public opinion that only the men could ride off on an Ade. When told that women could only ever be camp followers, she had drawn her bow, sighted on the wall map and let fly an arrow into the heart of Ka, the country presently (much to its distress) being Aded.

"I will fly just as sure and true into the heart of this heathen land," she declared. "My arrows will bring salvation, my stallion's hooves shall devour the desert." She was awfully difficult to dissuade, and quite loud. Her advisors hedged.

"You can't bring your Orse. He'd be eaten by hungry soldiers on the voyage there."

"They have fine horses in Ka, also very nice jewelry. But the wrong god. They must be saved." Lucia rejoined tartly. "When I return victorious I will bring some foreign Orses back for breeding stock and also gold, and the monastery of the Lattein order will be even more richly endowed. Offer me no advice, for I keep my own counsel. Fortune and glory await!"

"Fortune and er, glory!" the monks tried to sound cheerful. After all, many Aders were blessed by martyrdom.

There was indeed much martyrdom on both sides, but not for Lucia. Her headstrong attitude was her preservation on many occasions during the one-year Ade, or, as Pol called it, the Scardue, "because it's all mixed up" he would say in his old-soldier way.

In times of unrest among the Aders, skirmishes with the heathen, confounded communication and countermanding orders, Lucia often took control. It was this as much as her lovely singing voice, with which she would favor the men some evenings before sleep, that drew the Bishop to her against both the edicts of his church and his own best interests. He would never forget the first night he'd heard her sing, how it had laid waste the laws of his life, though the song itself had been nothing but a pretty lay with a happy ending, which was always the Aders' preference.

Bish had, shocked rigid in his blanket on the still-warm sand, known then he wanted always and only to follow that voice, strengthening its vessel until its radiance spilled over the enshadowed world, illuminating a shining path from each ignorant, earthly creature to the divine.

She really was quite a good singer.

The Bishop began to live for night, when she would bard for them lying lonely, a travel-sized harp they'd stolen for her sweetening her voice with its own. The nights she did not play, from fatigue or paining wounds, were wakeful and eternal ones for the Bishop. He had watched her in the firelight, dark hair lost to the night surrounding her, angular face and shaping lips in shadow. He was sure the other men watched her as he did (though his intentions were far nobler, he knew), not that anyone attempted anything other than visual or verbal communication with Lucia since she had stated her boundaries rather succinctly with an overly-friendly fellow shortly after joining the company.

Her voice on the other hand was a gift she offered them freely, and they had slaked themselves on its honey. After months lost in the wasteland, their position unrecognizable save for the clues found in their attackers' dress ("Banooly, did you see the amber?

We must be near Hab." "No good, the Banooly are nomadic in the Dust Season, we could be anywhere."), the Aders were becoming a bit sand-crazy, as though the sharp, burrowing grains that found their way into the Aders' socks, saddles, blankets, pantaloons, jerkins, weskits, chausses, codpieces and other food, and every ferd-given crevice in their ferd-given bodies, had also made their insidious, insatiable way into the Aders' brains.

When the Bishop first went in Sane,
he did not know himself to be there,
and assumed he was dreaming,
for there he saw,
in a fantasy of watercolor
flowers and long soft skin,
Lucia.
Though she
did occasionally metamorphose
into sequences of odd configurations and once,
to the Bishop's disgust,
his mother,
Rick and mostly Lucia
were in Sane together for ten days.
One full moon.
Five minutes. A lifetime.

The Aders had borne the febrile Bishop with them on their critical quest for an oasis, which Lucia had spotted with her sure-footed and motivated desert pony. After gaining a vantage point among jagged croppings of stone she was able to see far to the west where a smear of wavering green hovered above the combing dunes. During their stay at this oasis the Bishop recovered fully from his illness and resolved to press his case.

One night beneath a black colander of stars, shy moon creeping over the hills that cushioned Zappa, the Ader's target, the Bishop caught Lucia alone, the moon caught Lucia, Lucia caught the light and gasped sharply upon seeing the Bishop, dark robes in dark shadows under a palm. He pulled her gently into the darkness with him and whispered low in her ear of what he had seen while in Sane.

"I was there," she cried softly. "I've been there, crazy with this..."

"Love? Is it love?" demanded the Bishop.

"It was in Sane," Lucia said, "but it cannot be here. I am as a soldier to you whilst we campaign."

"What do you know of what can happen between soldiers?" he asked. Lucia blushed mauvely in the blue moonlight.

"Nonetheless, I have a Jeanne d'Arc thing going on here, and I can't be seen to...you know." The Bishop knew, all right, and one of the things he knew was that as soon as they all returned from the Ade, he was going to have himself defrocked, so to speak. The second thing he knew was that he was now on the look-out for a very special gift to keep himself foremost in the mind of his 'brother in arms'.

*   *   *

All was going according to the Cat's plan, as it had expected. As autumn settled more heavily around their abode, the Cat noticed an improvement in Pol's quality of attention to important things, like keeping the fire stoked, regular feeding-times and renewing the love-hate relationship the Cat had with its comb.

Alternately purring and growling menacingly, the Cat submitted itself to crude human-style grooming (though the comb did do a good job of the tricky bits under the chin and behind the head, granted). Now that the old man was free from the influence of the memory-bane, though a little winier, his original character was slowly beginning to reassert itself much to the Cat's relief. It seemed as good a time as any to tell Pol of the monks' plot.

Pol responded mildly to the news that he'd been systematically drugged for a dozen years, preoccupied with the mystery of why they'd felt the need to confuse him so.

"Twelve years, eh?"

"Yes, I figure it has to do with that woman you met on the fourth Ade, that singer. It was around then she 'disappeared'."

Pol ignored the Cat, rising laboriously from his chair (to the Cat's displeasure, for the combing was incomplete) and going to his archives. Three musty journals in cardinal, moss green and yellow leather were the Antiquarian's testament to the events of the year in question and he took them to his excitable desk to peruse them closely.

"Hmm. Trade increased with Pollonia, a Tract signed between the Connish princess and the Rade of Com..." He flipped pages. "...the five-legged frog is discovered on Thanksgiving Island, Eva Kent, bureaucrat, is crushed beneath a five-ton plasticslide, the five-legged frog is declared extinct, governmental confusion result of environmental toxicity..." He searched on, truly in his element. "Aha!" he exclaimed. He turned to the Cat triumphantly, bearing a curling news broadsheet whose headline read; 'Diva Shatters Priceless Harp, Disappears.' "I wonder if it might not be about this, and the various control issues of the (ahem) long lost Don Juana Lucia."

"Genius." muttered the Cat.

*   *   *

Bish enjoyed the expression on the poet's face upon discovering his patron in the room at the end of the hall, seated comfortably at table. Lit tapers high-set upon the wall in corroded sconces made sickly yellow shadows of the eerie darkness.

"Come in!" Bish invited jovially, rising as they entered. "I've brought a little cake for our celebration." The older man's square jaw forced itself into a beaming grin as he gestured to the delicious-looking seed cake on the table before him. "And who's your friend, Rex, would she like some cake too?"

"My name isn't Rex." Apt corrected, "And I'm fine for cake, thanks. Who are you?" She looked from the stranger to the poet, marking their similar features and the look of embarrassment on the poet's face.

"This is Bish O'Prick. He's my, my patron. He aids me in my search for the Harp." O'Prick bowed his head but kept his eyes upon Apt, his manner unreadable.

The poet seated himself as though hamstrung and took a piece of cake. "Lemon, my favorite."

"More of a financier than a patron I'd say, but call it what you will, he has been looking for the Harp for me since the time of its destruction."

"Looking for it...for you?" Apt's eyebrows raised uncomfortably. The poet nervously reached for another piece of cake.

"Why, yes," replied O'Prick. "When it's complete, he will bring it to me and I will pay him the agreed-upon sum. Isn't that right, boy?" The man looked over to the poet for confirmation, but the second piece had done him in, and Rex had fallen to the marble tiles.

Apt turned to O'Prick.

"You've killed him!" She grabbed the edges of the table as though to employ some of the fighting styles she'd seen demonstrated at the public houses. Bish cowered in his chair.

"No! Not dead! Don't hit, don't hit!"

"What have you done?" she demanded, looming above him. He relaxed a little as she released the table and was able to explain caustically,

"No more than any other true lover of music would do. I believed, and now you have proven to me, that he was planning to keep the Harp rather than give it to me as agreed." O'Prick fingered a medallion at his throat, an amulet of protection, Apt assumed. He'd better rub hard. O'Prick continued, "For reasons I won't get into, I am unable to find the Harp's parts myself and have need of the boy. He will overcome his selfish ploy and deliver the Harp to me perfected."

"He won't, he won't give it to you, you're no bard!" Apt declared, aware of a grinding metallic sound that she thought might be her clenching teeth. The man, suddenly assured, laughed at her fury, delectating over the mocking words,

"He will, he will deliver it freely though I think after all this perfidy that he won't be entitled to any further payment. He'll give it me all the same, though, and gladly."

"What makes you so sure?" Apt demanded. The shadows jumped around her as O'Prick leaned in closely to murmur,

"Because, my dear pawn, I'll have you." Two armor guards seized Apt, who, despite her struggles and angry shouts, was marched down to O'Prick's waiting carriage. Bish, remaining behind, nudged the poet's still form with the turned-up toe of his slipper.

"Have no fear my boy, I will take good care of your lady love until you return to me with the Harp." He instructed the empty men to remove the poet from Don Juana Lucia's summer palace, and gazed around at the room that he had helped design for her a seeming lifetime ago. "Soon, my love," Bish promised, "soon we will reunite, and you will sing once more."

Chapter 9

As the carriage departed, Bish succumbed to the eternal antagonistical temptation, and revealed to his captive audience the master plan. Apt, trussed, blindfolded and gagged, this last due to her steadfast refusal to stop yelling and thus interfering with Bish's storytelling, was compelled to listen. She would have called them the rantings of a madman save for the fact that they were decidedly not in Sane, and his speech was cogent, the story fluid, as though he had told it to himself on many long, solitary nights until it rang with verity.

"The Harp is mine, to use as I will. I rescued it from the deeps. I placed it in the ivory hands of Lucia where it lived as a temple of her voice until the world loved her more than I could. Her fame was staggering and she was offered everything, like royalty only better, for she was untetherable. Jewels were like candies to her, the embroidery on her hem blinded. It seemed she did not sleep, but only danced, sang, hunted and feasted. I saw her less and less as the world courted her. She for whom I had given up everything began to receive me in her parlor instead of her bedroom, then came the day when her servant returned with his silver tray, my calling card untouched on its rich surface and his carefully blank face telling me that I would see her no more, she was indisposed...to me, that is.

"It could be that I reminded her of being up to her elbows in heathen blood, of weeks bathing only in sand, of singing for lonely soldiers around a dung fire. Or that she was now simply too busy to pursue further the tender expressions that had passed between us upon returning from the Ade. We were happy, I assure you, in simplicity at first. Then came the sad tale all lovers tell, the pain of indifference in one's heart's desire, more fatal to affection than ire or jealousy, a true betrayal of promises believed at the time of making.

"Her music was all to her, and fairly so, to hear her sing was to fall into the ocean. Her music was all to me, and I freely gave myself to her as fodder for it, but I know in my soul that it was our love, and not the Harp, that brought her greatness."

The carriage spun slowly through harsh country, a thick rain like oil falling heavy on the sparse brush by the roadside. Apt wished herself wandering lost through these stony crags rather than trapped in the carriage with this villain, though she found her interest awakened by Bish's declamations on the nature of his love.

"I will remember always her face when she first saw the Harp. I had borne it with me from Ka, hidden from her with difficulty. I delayed presenting it until we were both settled again and I was a secular man in common clothes that have never felt truly right to me after the majesty of my robes. Nonetheless I was eager to begin our lives together freed from all vows but those I made to her. I saw, in her own precious face, barely scarred from all our adventures, her love. I felt that it was for me, with the Harp a mere token of the true gift.

"We were in Sane in the home we'd designed and built together, that you were in today. It's changed little in the last dozen years, a few staircases that weren't in the original plans, and an extra floor, but that room where I so surprised our young friend has altered not at all, so you may easily imagine how it was.

"I entered the room silently. This was her studio, her private place and I had never been inside. She had no reason to suspect my presence and continued the demanding practice to which she was increasingly committed. No one who hears a talented singer perform would ever imagine the caca- and poly-phonous vocalizations that occur behind the scenes, nor wish to. They are both horrible to hear and horrible to practice, and her concentration was total. I was able to stand the Harp upon the table behind her and conceal myself behind a drape. It was about an hour later, I'd guess, when she turned in frustration from a cracking treble note and beheld the Harp.

"I witnessed her incredulity, fierce surprise at this manifestation. She seemed angry until she found the note. I recall its wording: 'Great love hath made this Harp/to sing of love eternal/I give it you as a gift/to make it live and all that hear you/ever dream of the divine.'

"She laughed at the verse, but laughter stilled as she touched the Harp. I stepped from behind the curtain as her skillful fingers drew forth the first note and so the Harp and I were, in that moment, one to her... though it was only later I knew what a malediction that was."

Bish paused. "It's raining again," he muttered, and reached through the window to bang roughly on the carriage's side and bellow to the drivers to hurry up before the roads washed away. As the carriage jolted forward, Apt's face was thrown against the streaming window, her blindfold dislodging itself enough to permit her a look at the switchback road they'd just climbed. A lone figure on a lone Orse was following them, drenched in mud and rain but bearing a resilience that woke with hope Apt's own bound spirit.

Bish continued. "The tale is known by all, I hear, of how she swept in the turn of her skirts the crowned heads and commoners' alike as they fell at her feet. She ruled the world of song, becoming ever more forgetful of the debt she owed me. Voice, O vice the avid diva avoideth." O'Prick looked away, then resumed, musingly,

"Soon she will sing again. One cannot run away from fame, it is fame that causes the very thought of 'away' to evanesce, an illusion. There is no escape for her, though she may believe herself safe after these long years and my fruitless searching. But the Harp will call her to me and then it will call her back to the world, and she will cease this selfish isolation. She must be heard: all tongues hold song in her presence, so she must sing for them. We will find her together, the Harp and I. One string more, and the balance will tip," He gazed at Apt speculatively. She could feel but not see his eyes on her as the murmurous liturgy softened to a whisper quite close to her ear. "and you, pretty ransom, will bring it me." O'Prick laughed wickedly as Apt shivered with loathing.

The carriage pulled into a porte-cochere and Apt was dragged into the house and taken down a dank corridor, her blindfold and ropes removed so that she was able to see the dim dungeon awaiting her. She wrestled in the drivers' hold (it did take two of them to restrain her) to no avail; she was cast, sprawling into the reeking cell, whose small, barred window only made the shadows deeper. Apt was left, pounding already-roughened hands against a wooden door that stabbed her fists with splinters.

*   *   *

Gies and Essji were both angry and disconsolate. It was a dusty, ratty, stinky and occasionally squelchy business that sat not well with them but still they searched the acres of catacombs in the name of the poet and the love they bore his art. They pored through each nasty nook and crumbling cranny and found many strings, and things that looked like strings but weren't. However, none of them had the markings the poet had instructed them to look for.

"We'll"

"Never find it." they chanted, alternating the parts. In irritation, Essji pawed at a pile of helmets, which tumbled with an outlandish amount of noise as the twins froze. Time passed with no reprisal so they reluctantly initiated a perusal of the helmets, many of which contained deceptively stringy things, so they were preoccupied when a firm, elderly voice behind them demanded to know their purpose here. What it actually said was: "Oy!" in a particularly interrogative manner.

Gies and Essji spun, spent helmets falling from fingers splayed identically in fear, almost laughing in relief to see a sinewy man, quite alive, an enhackled Cat at his side. Their mirth was contained only by their fatigue, the consecrated setting and their slow but appreciative observation of the rather large sword brandished by a withered arm now made strong with fury.

They spoke nearly, sotto voce,

"D'you see"

"that sword?"

"Ader's sword"

"no doubt." They stepped apart slowly, and back one step just to be on the safe side. The Cat eyed them menacingly. Gies spoke calmingly, using honorifics,

"Most Valuable Veteran, Sir," he began. As the Cat grurrled, Essji took over:

"We mean no harm. We are sent on an honorable quest, and have not come to with base intent to plunder this holy place." The Cat growled louder, the blade lifted to a more lethal-looking angle at such a disparagement of plundering. The knightly image (if one were to imagine a knight bent and bowed, eighty or so, and the Cat as an Orse, ornately caparisoned) bade them say more of their goal.

"Really, not much, just a wee string." The man, regarding the twins meaningfully, allowed the blade to rest on its point between his knobbly bare feet.

"A string you say?"

"Aye, just the one."

"T'wouldn't be the string to Don Juana Lucia's Harp, would it?" The old man grinned. "You'd better come upstairs for some tea, the stone is aching my feet." Gies and Essji gaped, allowing themselves to be directed. The Cat, seeming to nod in agreement, might also have been chuckling in amusement as it followed the men through the catacombs.

*　　*　　*

Apt was desolate. There was something very wrong with O'Prick's plan for the Harp and Lucia, and she was at a loss to prevent her own use as bait. How could she face imprisonment? What if her abductor thought she might know of the string's location? Could she face torture? Could she face...

Could she face? Not just face but head, not just head but neck shoulders and all the rest? There was something in here about, what was it? She gently withdrew from the inner pocket of the tunic given her by the sistaz a now considerably battered folio whose papers were not improved for their journeys, but still readable. Ah yes, something about snakes...

Removing her tunic with the folio in its pocket and placing it sensibly on the ledge between the bars, Apt rested her chin on the edge of the window and gave herself a serpent's face. Most any child with clay would tell you snakes are easy to make and it's true in terms of the shape, but this was the most difficult thing Apt had ever done and it pinched quite a bit. She worked silently for what felt like hours. It would have been torture except that she was choosing to do it, was doing it, was successfully winding her long, light-green patterned head and not-shoulders-anymore out over the dank stone wall of her prison into the cloudy twilight beyond.

Where Asp noticed that the prison backed directly onto a sharp cliff, sloping steeply and far down to the crashing river below. Grateful for her prehensile tail and circumstantial circumference, she offered herself inch by inch to the thin grip of ground along the foundation. She was flat out, and needed to rest. She slept.

*   *   *

Peaceful ease descended also upon the Antiquarian's abode, where those assembled had been introduced over some tea which was a bit unusual. Pol had said this was how they'd done it in the Ade, though how they'd gotten their hands on sphagnum moss in the desert of Ka, the twins were too polite to ask. Seated around the fire, most welcome on a miserable night like this, they made small talk until the tea had been dealt with as was polite, then got right to it. There were many Buthowdids and Wheredidits and other questions on both sides, as the Antiquarian was unaware that the parts of the Harp had been collected, and he had a certain interest in the subject.

"Buthowdid you know we were looking for the Harp string?"

"What other string could bring two lads to such unlikely circumstances?"

"Doyouknow where it is?" asked Essji bluntly. The cat stretched appreciatively in the Antiquarian's lap, vibrating with merriment.

"A fine question." Pol settled in for the discourse. "D'you mean where it is, or where it should be? Or one could argue that it is where it's supposed to be even if it isn't where it should be, don't you think?"

"Man, we need to know where it's at!" Essji exploded.

"Don't we all?" The Antiquarian said musingly, then noticed the looks on the twins' face and declared, "I will tell you a story." The twins exchanged glances. "A short story." Relieved glances.

"Does it have a happy ending?" asked Gies, anticipating the worst.

"It's never everybody's happy ending." Pol replied, and began his tale.

*   *   *

Was she still dreaming, Asp wondered waking into deeper darkness. A small, gentle voice spoke as though right by her ear, which it was. Nestled in the clammy stone wall were some interestingly-capped mushrooms, one of which was inclined conversationally towards her. She scented the air with her tongue; at least the talking fungus wasn't toxic.

"I didn't catch that." Asp hissed with some hesitation. While she had not considered that she would converse with a mushroom, her serpentine perspective indicated the wisdom of listening.

"I said, you'd better wake up, I think they've found you out." the mushroom whispered. Indeed, a screech could be heard from within the fortress.

"WHERE IS SHE?" Déjà déjà vu, Asp thought, quickly considering her options. She could put on a cliff face, they'd look right past her, but on the other hand they likely wouldn't look for her out here at all, especially as a snake.

"Why am I here?" she hissed.

"Not my department, ask your life's porpoise." replied the mushroom.

"What's your department, then?" inquired Asp.

"I'm the morel of the story."

"Oh yes, what do you do?"

"I morelize, like this: *Don't judge a book by its cover. Look within yourself for the treasure you seek. You know you're lucky if people help you when you ask.*"

"Very nice, any others?"

"Yes, *If you wish to retain possession of your property, you should remove it from the window before the guards notice it.*" With horror, Asp observed her tunic, draped over the windowsill far above.

"Could you give me a boost?"

"Only morel support," said the mushroom sadly.

"It's just that if I stop being a snake, I'll fall off the edge. But if I don't change, then they'll find the folio, and I won't be able to keep my promise. It's a morel dilemma."

"It isn't." sniffed the morel. *"Just be yourself."*

Aspt be'd, attaining fingers and arms while still resting her lower coils on the strip of earth. She grasped the tunic just as her, oh dear, feet!

slipped. The morel appeared to wave cheerily as she plummeted.

This was not friendly-though-high-impact lake water, this was a river that fought with her on entry and attempted Apticide by battery and drowning. Already long past tired, Apt wasn't much of a sparring partner, and felt a comfort calling from deep under the white water which gleamed in the night as she drowsed, just one more ripple, slipping beneath the surface.

*   *   *

By the time the tale was told, it was the middle of the night, though it was a rather short version of the story by the Antiquarian's standards. Gies and Essji were invited and elected to remain the night, the Cat graciously offering them its spot by the fire. They woke simultaneously in the night with a sense of being part of something larger than themselves (which was quite a stretch), and also an even stronger sense that the Cat was lying across them contentedly. They whispered to each other so as not to disturb it.

"We've got to get word"

"back to Rex"

"tell 'im what we learned."

"Should we"

"go now? Waste no"

"time like the present." Gies yawned. Every muscle in his considerable body was aching, craving rest, and he could reasonably assume that his brother's condition was similar if not identical. Nonetheless he started to sit up and was halted by a casual paw extended by a particularly comfortable and intricately arranged feline.

"Sleep." whispered the Cat, eyelids hypnotizingly at half-mast.

"I think we'd better do what it says." Essji muttered. Gies agreed. They were asleep again too soon to hear the Cat purr,

"Yes, that's right. Do what the Cat says." as it settled even more deeply into its twin bed.

*   *   *

The midnight river was not as strong as Anenome, who found it a pleasant playmate and had so much fun among its tickling rills that she almost forgot to retrieve Apt. It was tricky, maintaining her freshwater skin and maneuvering the limp human downstream, but no more challenging really than a sodden couch, and Anenome wielded Apt easily once she got the hang of her.

Attending to the leg walker once she was at least half on shore was simple enough after Anenome figured out that the air went in the nose or mouth. Apt was bruised, with a voice that sounded like the river had actually gone right though her, but breathing.

"You saved me!" Apt grasckled wonderingly. "Howdidyou..."

"My podmate was morelly obliged to let me know you'd fallen. You held your own until I could get to you. Now you're safe, and with your true love." Apt tried to sit up, didn't.

"What?" Apt gaspailed. Anenome looked fishily surprised.

"The poet is camped over there." With a fin she pointed out the glow of a campfire down the riverbank a distance. "He's been waiting for you, having heard of your daring escape." Apt hoped this was not the case, considering how she'd scaled her prison wall. She thought he might have been unable to reach her by the perilously steep and muddy roads and, feeling a tad sulky or perhaps also drugged, had gone to find a nice spot by the river. "He is your true love, isn't he? That is why I took him to you in Con and why I saved you."

"I know that at this moment, I am cold and wet, though alive, thanks to you, your podmate and some morel guidance, and the poet has a fire, tea, blankets. Presently, that is what I love and if he'll share them, who knows?"

Anenome dove back into the torrent, muttering something about that it wasn't at all like in the romance novels, and Apt agreed, sore from toes to the crown of her head.

He was exhausted too, she could tell as she approached. She also knew he thought he was dreaming as she came closer to him in the darkness.

"Is that you, lassie?" he asked, voice shaking. If Apt could have spoken, her own would also have trembled with cold and joy overwhelming as he pulled back the blankets to welcome her inside.

Chapter 10

Morning came too early for the weary twins but the Anti-quarian was cheerful on this rare sunny day as they readied themselves for the journey back to De, where Rex would meet them as arranged.

"If I were a younger man I'd go along with you, never been to De, t'was an Ade before my time, left the inhabitants in a bit of a pickle, I understand. They often do. I was in Ed though, for the 7ᵗʰ Ade, razed the cities to the ground. No real harm done, though, Ed isn't well known for its history. Not like..."

Gies turned slowly from his inspection of their gear and looked stolidly at the old man with an expression that miraculously quelled the edifying stream of words. Then he smiled.

"You are indeed an M.V.V., sir. I fain would come to hear your wisdom again."

"And welcome." The Antiquarian bowed his head graciously, a pencil sketch in the milk-grey dawn. "You'll remember what I told you?"

"Only half, but"

"I'll remember the other half." finished Essji.

"Good, good. You must find a way to keep Lucia out of the Bishop's hands, and find Apt, for she holds the key, so to speak. Go now in peace my friends, and come again soon. And next time please bring more of those bird's-nest cookies."

The brothers so promised and departed with two of the Antiquarian's 27 Orses, having dismissed the camels, llamas and a single-horned Orse as unsuitable mounts. Pol watched them ride away into the distance. He saw for a moment pennants snapping in a dust storm around them as they bore inexorably down on their target with will squared and wished himself a younger man, riding again.

The Cat, impatiently knocking against the Antiquarian's shins, mrowed inquisitively.

"They'll be back, small cat, and I will be not unhappy to see them. Perhaps they'll come back with this poet, and we shall hear some ballads," Pol noticed the Cat's tail twitch aggressively, "or not."

"As long as they bring those cookies."

*　　*　　*

Rays of light struck Apt's eyelids. Morning! There was something, somebody...oh yes, the poet, who lay on his side, one arm over her hip. By the expression of perfect repose on his face, he was more comfortable than she felt. Apt's body felt as though it had been put inside a large iron drum and rolled down an extremely long and bumpy hill. She moved effortfully and gently so as not to disturb him. She was enjoying this tranquil moment as the sun more fully embraced the verdant glen, finding the two where they lay and bathing them in radiant light, the river also sparkling by, her lover peacefully dreaming beside her, slowly opening his beautiful blue eyes and focusing in on her, like a kitten. His sensuous mouth parted.

Apt was unprepared for the poet's yelp as he struggled up and away from her.

"Who are you?" he demanded. "Why don't I remember you?"

"I came to you last night in the darkness, perhaps you were sleeping and that is why you remember me not."

"Why did you come? Are you from one of the pubs? Was I drunk?"

"I'm Apt!" said Apt.

"For what?"

"No, that's what I'm called."

"Never heard of you." the poet retorted, rolling his blankets, kicking at the last embers of the fire, untethering his Orse. Apt was shocked.

"Where are you going?"

"There's a lass in trouble up that mountain. Now that the rains have stopped, I should be able to get up there. I only hope I'm not too late."

"But I, I mean, she, I..." Bewildered, Apt rubbed at her forehead. Something was wrong. "I'm her, the lass. I got away." The poet looked at her reproachfully.

"I don't care about your way, you're not her so quit your pretense."

"But I am!" Apt exclaimed. "I met you at the Open Hart, you tended my wounds..." Her hand again found the smooth skin of her forehead, near the right eye. Ah. She twined a finger in a red curl of hair and pulled it to where she could see it. What did she look like now? The poet was saddling his Orse, but stopped as she told him more of their adventures together. Arrested, he came close to her and looked deep into her brown eyes.

"How could it be true?" he wondered. His hand came to her face, still bruised from the river, and touched the unscarred flesh at her right temple.

"It is true. Do not look at me as though I am a stranger to you, for only the surface is changed." Apt

115

said. The poet's hand moved, a different expression in his eyes.

"I will need to know you again, then."

Apt's tale went untold for a considerable amount of time. The Orse, still saddled, munched hay unconcernedly nearby.

When words began to return to the pair, Apt told the poet of how she had come to be at the Open Hart, of her escape from the boss' wrath, her theft of the folio whose contents had enabled both her original disguise and her escape from O'Prick's clutches. The poet listened attentively, occasionally kissing her bare shoulder or toying with her curls (but not in the annoying way that people do, breaking the curl up and pulling it straight so that it becomes one mass of frizz-power, no, he did it nicely, content to feel the silken spiral around his fingers).

"...so," Apt concluded, "in my haste to become something tallish with fingers so that I could grab my tunic, I did not have the opportunity to select my appearance before falling from the cliff, and the events since had put all thought of it from my mind. If there were a still pool, I could look."

"I've a mirror," stated the poet "if you'd like to see." He rummaged in the nearby bag and extracted a shaving mirror.

Apt regarded her true face. It had been months since she'd seen herself. Apparently the morel's last aphorism (or were aphorisms a different species altogether?) had been taken more literally than intended. It was nice that the poet seemed to have taken it in stride, anyway, but Apt thought she'd miss her cat-green eyes. No matter, it felt good to be back in her skin, she decided. The poet requesting to see the folio,

Apt withdrew the poor thing from her sensible inner pocket and handed it to him delicately.

"It's amazing you held on to it through everything."

"I had to, I promised the Antiquarian I'd return it, that and the key to his dresser which I purloined. It's terrible when you lose the key to a drawer, so I do want to bring that back as well." The poet had removed the bedraggled pages, and tilted the folio over his hand. The key slithered into his palm, nesting upon the loops of its silvery filament.

After the poet had jumped up and down whooping for a while, he explained to Apt that this was the Harp string, the last, and now all they needed to do was return to De where Gies and Essji would meet them with the Harp's pieces. The Orse was saddled again, and almost convinced of the wisdom of taking two passengers, when the clank of armor alerted the pair to the presence of Bish O'Prick.

"A charming story," he sneered, "but not as sweet as the tale that will be told of how I brought Don Juana Lucia from hiding and returned her to her Harp and to the world, not half as endearing as the great love story that will be sung of for centuries to come. It will be my story, mine and Lucia's, that bards ornament with music and verse. It will, I think, not be the tale of a lack-luster poet and his false-faced stable girl." He laughed, clapping his hands as an order to seize the two. As the guards stepped a pace forward, heavy-footed and seemingly hesitant to acquit their orders, Apt noticed a scaly form behind them.

It was Anenome, who tripped, tugged and tossed into the torrential river each of the three guards in turn before O'Prick had really registered her arrival. She remedied his oversight by repeating her successful method on him, stopping short of the final, wet step. O'Prick was dumped unceremoniously on his behind at the very edge of the river, where the angry creature rose above him, balanced on her muscular tail.

"I was a fry when you came through the sea in your submarine, when you stole from our museum the Hornwhale Harp. As I grew, my pod shared news of its use in the world above, and we let you live, for seafolk are even more susceptible to the charms of music than humanity, and Lucia's music was very fine, and you were a-musing for her. But when your "love" pushed her deeper into the world and even undersea dwellers could see she was drowning, we began to know that this was not a love story.

"It was your greed that broke Lucia's voice and scattered the bones of the Harp and now you plot to flush her out with it? It will not be so, thief." O'Prick stood in terror, riveted by Anenome's ocean-aged eyes. "You have work to do below the surface, you will come down with me and Fluisa's spirit will rest. When the Harp is returned to us (she looked meaningfully at Apt and the poet), you will see it again, hear it played again sometimes after your long, awful labors. It will become clear to you that your love was not for Lucia." The Un-Undine paused, reviewing the quaking mound of terrestrial flesh before her. "Who knows? You might even be happy." she seemed to smile, fish-jaws separating, then finned a curiously unresisting O'Prick and leapt with him into the current that would bear them out to sea.

The poet shook himself.

"Did you see that?" he asked. Apt was silent, thoughtful. The poet scrabbled for his book and immediately began making notes.

"How were you planning on getting to De from here? We're hours from the coast." asked Apt. The poet wrote faster.

"Didn't have a plan really." scribble scribble "thought we might" scribble "get a lift with the Undine" scribble scribble scribble, scratch, scratch, scribble, sigh "but she's obviously busy. You got any ideas?" scribble.

"We could try a life porpoise." said Apt. "I have no idea what mine is, but you seem fairly clear on the topic. Maybe if you were to focus on how it will feel to complete your restoration of the Harp. Think of your porpoise." The poet leaned gently upon the Orse's side with a pleased expression.

"That's a good plan." He closed his eyes.

It did take awhile, because he kept getting distracted. Finally, after the poet had sat down, wrapped himself in a blanket, removed his boots and socks, put the book and pen in the bag, sat down again and spent a good many minutes in thought, the porpoise appeared. They could only ride with it as far as the coast, for the porpoise did not have a command of freshwater and saltwater skins like Anenome, and they'd need to free the Orse (which pleased Apt), but they knew they would travel safely, on porpoise.

After a slippery and playful water voyage for the porpoise and a stony, turbulent nightmare for its passengers, the porpoise nosed its limp cargo onto the riverbank and was weakly thanked. After Apt and the Poet had regained themselves, they sought passage on a ship to De, where their sodden appearance was noticed but not remarked upon by the sailors.

*　　*　　*

Upon barking, the pair was much improved, and to their light, Gies and Essji were at the dock to meet them. Receiving congratulatory and overly enthusiastic claps on the back from the twins for their success in the string's recovery, they returned to the sistaz' town home, during which journey the twins reported the information they'd received from the Antiquarian, of whom Apt was pleased to hear that he was well.

"So Lucia's still alive,"

"lives yet in a hamlet a day's ride"

"from Bonhomie, near the catacombs. She and the Antiquarian"

"Pol"

"Were on Ade together, that's where she met the"

"Bish O'Prick"

"and when she got too famous"

"the Antiquarian helped her destroy the harp and helped her hide by"

"changing her face"

"so nobody knew that she was Don Juana Lucia"

"even tho' she socializes a lot, holds parties, grand hunts, that"

"sort of thing."

Apt interrupted.

"Hunts?"

"Yep,"

"birds mostly, songbirds, I guess"

"she doesn't like to hear the singing." finished Apt, the twins looked at her quizzically. "Did Pol tell you her name? Was it Raph?"

"T'was." Gies admitted wonderingly. Apt turned to the poet.

"My boss, ex-boss I should say. She used to fire people for humming. I should have known."

"Often things are hidden in plain sight." the poet replied.

The twins said there was more to tell, and revealed the Cat's discovery of poisoning. The Antiquarian had duced that Raph herself had been behind it. Fearing for his disclosure of her true identity and that he would someday seek the Harp's resurrection, she had arranged with the Lattein monks to dose his food with Obscurata, thus keeping him unreasonable. This is why Apt had found him so unlike himself upon fleeing the big house.

She leaned against the seat, an ultimate luxury after her recent modes of transport, and thought of how complex the past becomes when it becomes right now. The cadent city passed by outside the coach's windows as they approached the townhouse.

As soon as they arrived and told Mentia and Lirium of their victory, the sistaz left, having no sire to inadvertently be healed of their respective conditions by an overly-sanitary harp.

"It would be meaning." Mentia said, pausing before Apt to examine her altered appearance.

"Well, you're a shape shifter, at least that's something different. The others he's brought by were distressingly normal." clared Mentia.

"Prosper Well." said Lirium, quite lucidly. It sounded to Apt like goodbye.

The Harp was assembled, its final string thread and tuned (which process had made the party glad of an abundant stock of cotton batting found in the kitchen), and the Harp awaited its test. The poet looked at Gies and Essji. He imagined them good-humored, affable and pleasant, as the Harp would make them with its correcting harmonics. He hesitated.

"Maybe you two should wait downstairs."

"But we've waited so long to hear you play it! It's all we've worked for, for years!" said Essji hotly.

"He's probably afraid." Gies moped. "Maybe he thinks if he plays it he'll fall under its spell, and it'll be his curse as it was hers." Actually, the poet hadn't considered that aspect. He regarded the Harp.

Freshets of carved bone arched upwards from the base, the strings were a dewy web of light. The poet's fingers itched. What if he were to fulfill O'Prick's intention, carry this Treasure back to Don Juana Lucia and call her forth? Or take it himself to the Crystalphan City, the heart of musical civilization in their realm, and make his entrance on the world stage, armed with an unstoppable weapon? He felt an urgent tug on his sleeve.

"What are you thinking?" asked Apt, an edge of something in her voice. "You're looking a bit like the bad guy did, just around the eyes." The poet turned to her, and to her surprise, burst into tears. Apt requested a moment of privacy which request was gladly honored by the discomfited twins, and she was left alone with the poet. She held him until he was able to speak.

"I want to play it!" he cried.

"So play it." Apt said, agreeably.

"I'm scared to play it."

"Why are you frightened, poet? Is this not what you've worked your whole life for? Why should you stop now?" she asked. The poet gazed into her eyes with ineffable sadness.

"I'm afraid that it won't be worth it. I mean, what song can I play on an ancient Harp made from an extinct whale, stolen from the Undines a generation ago? Should it be 'Molly's Cakewalk' or 'Spang Goes the Breastplate? There's nothing important for me to say. It's my life's porpoise, I've attained it, and now what? There's nothing noble left on my list of things to do."

Apt considered carefully.

"There is something." she murmured.

*　　*　　*

"Will ye not come with us, lass?" asked Gies as Essji and the poet loaded the last of their gear onto the boat. Maibaybi was a distant desert country and much equipment was needed for their journey to the faraway home of the great courtesan Lentdemain who, according to the ship's captain, still clung to life.

"Nay," replied Apt, with some regret, eyeing the strong form of the poet as he bent to his labors. "I made a promise, several actually, and I must return the key and folio to Pol. Perhaps when you return to Bonhomie you will pass by, and tell me of your adventures."

"T'be sure" Gies began. Essji and the poet joined them. The sailors were beginning to cast off.

"you can bet on it." finished Essji. Embracing Apt, they departed to load the remainder of their goods. Apt and the poet were left alone among the crowds of travelers and their well-wishers.

"I'll miss you, lassie." The poet whispered close to her ear as he hugged her. Apt's eyes smarted, but she drew away to look at him, blurred a little against the wide blue expanse.

"Me too. Good luck to you in Maibaybi, I have a feeling that the Harp will do Lentdemain wonders... just watch out that they don't offer you a post as head eunuch as a reward!" The poet smiled.

"I'll be careful."

"And you'll remember to return the Harp to the Undines as soon as you're done at the palace?" Apt asked pointedly.

"I thought I might hold on to it for a bit. Bring it back to the Terrible Boar, show me mum."

"Or?"

"Or I could just return it to the Undines. Probably a better idea."

"Especially since I let Anenome know where you were heading." Apt warned in a friendly manner.

"Especially because of that." the poet grinned.

Rising in the briny air, a chorus of horns called the passengers. For a moment sensing the poet becoming closer, a brush of lips on her unscarred forehead, and then only the feeling of his becoming further and further away. Apt did not watch the ship as it pulled from the docks, did not see the poet and the twins wave from the deck, did not stand and stare after it. By the time it passed out of sight on the horizon, Apt had already booked a first-class ticket, compliments of the sistaz' generosity, and boarded her own vessel bound for Bonhomie.

Epilogue

Apt had moved her Queen unwisely, and the Antiquarian was savoring the possible consequences of this for Apt's undefended Knight as the lovely spring passed unnoticed outside.

Apt had returned the key and the folio (along with a very nice copy she'd done herself on heavy, water-repellent stock in case of future adventure) and the Antiquarian had received them with kindness and curiosity as to her use of them. Her changes and travels had offered some amusing anecdotes for the Antiquarian's records, not that Apt had told him everything that had occurred.

Pol had offered her a post as Chief Orser for his herd of 47 Orses and comfortable accommodations near the stables, which Apt had accepted with pleasure as her days were now spent mostly in the riding and training of Orses and supervising of the stable hands who took care of mucking out the stalls (though never into the river) and other dirty jobs. She spent her considerable free time at the Terrible Boar with Bess, having long, earnest conversations with its patrons about respectful water use. Apt and the Antiquarian saw each other infrequently, most often for meals which were now lavish and being provided with gratitude by the monks of the rose and lily, who knew of Pol and Apt's roles in Lentdemain's miraculous cure. They also met for the occasional game.

Chess was a re-discovered passion, and as usual, the Antiquarian was taking it to the extreme. Pouring more dark tea from the samovar, Apt interrupted Pol's reverie in Russian, the language of the house at present and one in which she was enjoying considerable fluency.

"Pol?"

"Hm?"

"Do you still remember my original name?" The Antiquarian looked over the top of his glasses at the young woman before him.

"Yes." he said curtly, moving his Knight to fork both Apt's Knight and Rook. Apt reviewed the new position. After a time, he asked, "Did you want me to tell you?" Eyes on the board, she smiled.

"No, I think I don't." She moved her Queen. "In all these adventures, no matter what met me, I have proved myself to be Apt. So I shall remain. Check."

The Kot purred happily on Apt's lap.

The End

LaVergne, TN USA
02 April 2010
177935LV00001BA/8/P